THE DEVIL'S HUNTING GROUNDS

THE DEVIL'S HUNTING GROUNDS

HARRY BLAMIRES

Thomas Nelson Publishers
Nashville • Camden • New York

ISBN 0-8407-5932-0

Library of Congress Cataloging in Publication Data

Blamires, Harry.
  The devil's hunting grounds.

  Originally published: London: Longmans, Green, 1954.
  I. Title.
PS3503.L39D47   1984   813'.54   84-19048
ISBN 0-8407-5932-0

To
Ralph Ellis White

Foreword to edition of 1984

There is something to be said for a fresh introduction to a book that is reissued thirty years after its original publication. I had already written *The Secularist Heresy* (originally called *The Faith and Modern Error*) when I sat down to write *The Devil's Hunting Grounds*, but I had put the completed typescript in a cupboard and left it there, doubting whether straight theology would be readily acceptable from the pen of one who was neither a cleric nor an academic divine by profession. I thought that readers ought to be softened up before I confronted them as a lay theologian. so I launched myself into the field of theological fiction, attracted by the possibilities it offered for blending humour and satire with seriousness.

My aim was to contrast bad thinking with sound thinking in an amusing and ironic way. I started with this first-person record of a dream-pilgrimage through the hereafter in which a guardian angel is often at hand to put the pilgrim's earthbound notions straight. My novels were thus intended to be entertaining variants on the themes propounded in my more direct polemical works. After all, if a thing is worth saying, it is worth repeating. And we know from the Bible that the more valid a message is, the more variously repeatable it is. So, in this first novel, the pilgrim encounters people who peddle various modish perversions of Christian teaching which substitute sentimental altruism or vague uplift for full-blooded faith.

A writer always runs a risk when he mingles seriousness with humour. One of the book's earliest reviewers, the novelist Kinglsey Amis, wrote, "As a tract I don't think the book succeeds; as a satire I found it neat and amusing." It appeared to him that I had been more successful as an entertainer than as a man with a message. *The Times Literary Supplement* reviewer too said, "The satire is at its best when it is most earthly" but he then conceded: "As a sincere defence of Christian doctrine, and a plea for a return to authority in matters of belief, the book is clear and even dramatic in places."

When I stayed in Oxford with C. S. Lewis not long after the publication of the book, he tackled me about my handling of the narrator's guardian angel, Lamiel. I had tried to suggest authoritativeness in modern terms by giving the angel the idiom of the bureaucrat and the pedant. Why had I done this? Lewis asked. "I thought it funny," I said. "It is very funny indeed," Lewis grinned—but was I perhaps in danger of not treating angelhood seriously enough? He added that, when he first started to write *The Screwtape Letters*, his intention had been to balance the correspondence between devils attacking the human soul with correspondence between angels protecting him. But then he decided that it would be too presumptuous thus to try to enter the angelic mind. This, said with the utmost friendliness and good humour, certainly carried a probing point. It appeared that I had rushed in among the angels where Lewis had feared to tread.

Preliminary Admonition

As the reader knows full well that I have never visited the Supernatural Regions herein depicted, he may be equally assured that I have never met the persons residing there, except in imagination.

Any apparent resemblances to actual human beings, which the reader may fancy that he detects, are to be accounted delusions of the Devil, who loves thus to distract us from the main issues, by seducing us to invidious comparisons and malicious judgments.

The reader is exhorted, therefore, to resist these machinations of the Author of all Evil, who would blind us to the clear Light of Reason by the dark distraction of personal animosities.

The frontiers between sense and spirit
are the Devil's hunting-grounds.

COVENTRY PATMORE

1

"An angel! I had no idea..."

"Nevertheless I am," he said, and his eyes glanced backwards to the great wings overarching his head. I looked up at them in astonishment. Of course I had already seen them, but not as wings. In my stupidity I had not noticed that they were *connected* to him. I had thought that he stood there under the shelter of some great tree—some strange exotic palm. It had not struck me as incongruous that a tree should be silver-blue, for indeed I had often seen such colour effects on the stage.

"You find me rather too solid," he said; and I nodded.

"Perhaps even a little crude?"

I sensed laughter in his voice and I smiled sympathetically. It struck me that we shared a common sense of humour; and, as I looked up at him again, my smile laid claim to some degree of fraternal equality. But I had blundered. There was no laughter in his eyes; only an unflinching sternness, strangely tranquil, that stabbed to the heart.

"Confess," he said, "that you would be much more

comfortable if you could see right through me."

It was true; and I lowered my head.

"You are a child of your time. You never believed in ghosts, yet you pictured angels as transparent wraiths. You expected the real to be less substantial than the finite and the physical. You preserved a belief in supernatural beings by divesting us of substance. What you dared not deny, you mentally vaporized."

His sternness strangely emboldened me, and I tried to plead.

"I knew that you were not of the earth earthy."

"Not visible, not corporeal, not finite: in short, you were content to imagine us as bundles of nothingness. It comes to the same thing. Did it never occur to you that we might prefer to be opposed rather than vaporized, to be denied rather than negativized? I think you have known in your own way what it is to hunger for support—or even for opposition—and then to find yourself merely ignored. You have known what it is to yearn for a rational attack upon your opinions and sentiments, and then to find your most adverse intellectual foes treating you as though you fully agreed with them. Well, then, you have experienced vaporization yourself; and you found it the ultimate insult, the extremest humiliation. You smarted under it: yet you flung out the same mocking taunt upon us who have watched over you." There was a sudden sadness in his voice as he added, slowly and deliberately, "Perhaps you flung the insult further still."

I shuddered, and grasped desperately for words which might stem the flow of accusation. They came from me in a thoughtless cry—

"I see it all now."

"Don't talk like a third-rate novelist," he said

quickly, but not, I thought, in irritation. "You see it; but you certainly do not see it all. Nor will you for a long time yet. Meanwhile you have not asked my pardon."

"I'm sorry," I said; but it was clear to both of us that the words expressed bewilderment rather than penitence. They were received in silence, so I hastily added, "Naturally, I expected all that would come later and, well, not exactly elsewhere, but before..."

"Before Another," he said, "You wish to reserve all your penitence for one supreme moment of prostration before the Mercy Seat? The wish is not utterly unworthy; for indeed there are deep rejections of the past ahead of you, I hope. But the minor pin-pricks of injured social relationships must be dealt with first. I do not seek a confession from you. I am merely anxious that we should put ourselves on a proper footing with each other. That is a necessary preliminary if our relationship is to be fruitful, even here. So let us reach a proper understanding, for I may add that your dilatoriness in this respect is delaying our progress unwarrantably."

"I'm sorry," I said painfully. "And I beg your pardon. It is true that I never seriously took your existence into account, in my personal affairs at any rate. Please forgive me."

There was an awkward pause, as I stood before him, hanging my head, not daring to look up.

"Is that all?" he asked, still cold and remote. "Now that you grant my substantiality, is nothing else called for?"

Somehow I realized what he meant, and I sank onto my knees before him. His hands touched my head and at once I knew that I was in his keeping. I felt within me all the freshness and warmth of discovered companionship. Was this what I had idly thrown away below? Had all past loneliness been an unnecessary self-deprivation?

"You have our pardon, my child. Of course it is but the beginning. Or rather it is what enables us to begin. Come!"

He took my hand and raised me to my feet. And then we moved.

In order to give an impression of the way in which I moved, I should have to say that I ran; for indeed my legs went through the motions of running and my chest pressed forward. But no effort or weariness accompanied the movement, and the ground seemed resistless as surf. Moreover, conversation was just as easy as when we were stationary, and even more exhilarating. There was no longer any awkwardness. The angel became oddly apologetic.

"We Guardians are accustomed to difficulties in establishing contact with our wards; and as a result there are certain apparent inequalities in the reception of newcomers here. It is impossible for us to give overt assistance and visible companionship to wards who deny our existence. I will not say that support and friendship are necessarily less real—or less effective—when they are concealed. But there are obvious advantages in free communication, and we do not like to be denied it. We are not touchy beings, but we are incorrigibly logical, and definite preconditions must be satisfied before proper contact with us can be established. In particular we must be recognized to be no less formidably substantial than we indeed are."

"Does this mean," I asked "that you never appear before those who disbelieve in you?"

"It is not quite so bad as that. To begin with, I was speaking only of Guardians and their relations with their wards. Angels charged with official examining duties and the like inevitably face their charges openly. And we Guardians manage to make fitful open contacts with even the most obdurate wards; but it is rarely pleasant and often unfruitful."

I pulled lightly at his hand and said, "It would be impossible to doubt your substantiality in a situation like this."

"No man can be dragged thus through the air by a disembodied spectre. You are not engaged at the moment, therefore, in a great venture of faith. And I may as well tell you that, even in this little matter, you have not been an easy case. In a sense you have believed in us—and hence you have the good fortune to be at my side now. But there has been an implicit denial of substantiality in your imagining of supernatural beings. It was necessary to correct the error. You may rest assured that, for our part, we shall not refer to the matter again. Of course I cannot answer for any higher authority. For one thing, I do not clearly know the full extent of your fault in this direction, though it is a fault which some of us have to deal with only too frequently. We have come to expect it in a certain class of entrant. My own work is largely within the department which deals with the twentieth century, and we rarely receive anyone who is innocent in this respect. Other newcomers, from different centuries, have different problems, as you may imagine. My friend Alaziel, whose work falls within the thirteenth century, tells me that he had two good souls to receive yesterday whose trouble was quite the opposite of yours. As their Guardian, he found that they always kept an

empty bedroom for him, and laid an extra place at the
supper table. Alaziel was by no means displeased by
their attentive ministrations; but there was an error to
correct—an intellectual error. Not as serious as yours,
of course; but that is not entirely your fault. A man
cannot choose his own century; and we always reckon
the twentieth century to be an especially superstitious
one—at least compared to the thirteenth."

Now there were one or two things in the angel's
words which I found hard to digest. For instance, he
implied that the thirteenth century was at this moment as much within the scope of angelic scrutiny as
the twentieth. I had never been guilty, I hoped, of
conceiving eternity as mere after-life, as mere exten-
sion of time. The notion of an eternity which enclosed
and enfolded time had, in fact, always appealed to
me. But the idea of a state into which twentieth-century men could enter contemporaneously with men
from the thirteenth century came to me as a shock.

"Too crude again, in fact," the angel said, reading
my thoughts. "You tried to vaporize eternity too."

I was not too obtuse to appreciate the similarity of
my various delusions, so I tried to make amends.

"It must be difficult for newcomers from different
centuries to understand one another."

"They don't have to. You're jumping to unwarranted conclusions. I told you that work with freshers
is departmentalized. You will meet only your contemporaries at first: maybe you will never meet anyone
else."

I was relieved, though still mystified; and I turned
to another difficulty raised by the angel's words.

"Is *superstition* really the right word for the twentieth-century attitude to the supernatural?"

"I certainly can't think of a better. There is nothing more outrageously irrational—and, I may add, more shockingly unscientific—than the vaporized images in which your contemporaries indulge when they use the vocabulary of religion. Surely the supreme superstition is to conceive the real as less real than the finite."

"If you put it like that..." I began.

"I do put it like that. You have been granted a perfectly adequate set of words for discussing and picturing the supernatural. For simple people, uncorrupted by intellectual skepticism, the familiar stories and symbols readily convey the truths of Revelation. And in order to cater for meddlesome intellectuals, we allowed our great friend St. Thomas to establish the analogical validity of theological utterance beyond question for intelligent enquirers. Yet all your contemporaries can do is to vaporize theological images and destroy their symbolic content. They have learned to speak of heaven and hell, of angels and devils, and to mean nothing at all by their words. This is a matter which at our level, among the Hierarchies, is found particularly offensive. You must be very careful in your references to it when you converse with my colleagues. Some of the mildest and most patient find it difficult to restrain themselves on this issue alone. For one thing, this problem has added enormously to the strain on our already heavily-burdened educational system. We have always had plenty of beginners to deal with—souls utterly ignorant of the Faith in its rational aspect. Now we have too this appalling intake of baptized and supposedly taught souls who have mastered a religious vocabulary without imbibing a single clear and true conception of what it is they talk about. You see, in their condition on entry, these people are quite literally unteachable. There is no vocabulary with which one can approach them, since they are accustomed to annihilate the connotations of theological words in the very act of receiving them. We have to put the new entrants of this kind in special educational institutions, such as the College for Gnostics at Helicon. There they are left to themselves, on the whole. The hope is that they will gradually come to appreciate how threadbare their thinking is. Only then can we hope to instruct them. The worst cases go to Fordshaw. It may be that you will have to go there yourself for a course in the Backward Believers' Department."

"I'm sure I have a lot to learn," I said, anxious not to presume.

"True humility rarely expresses itself in phrases so unbearably trite," he remarked, "but we shall see."

I blushed as he thus shattered my sham platitude, and my hand trembled in his. He turned to look at me, as if weighing my discomfiture and scrutinizing my inner thoughts. Then, after a pause, he spoke again with an instructive air.

"I checked you once before for uttering a platitudinous cry which was intended to convey more than you truly felt. You must not abuse the spoken word when addressing angels. You must not, in your utterances, lay claim to virtuous feelings which are at present foreign to your disposition. No angel will be deceived by such pretences. The spectacle of a tongue erecting a façade before a mind is ridiculous and contemptible. Those new arrivals here who persist in representing themselves falsely through their own speech, in conversation with angels, are eventually deprived of all power of utterance. And it is a laborious business to renew in them the capacity for speech, as you will discover, if you come across our Department for the Education of the Dumb. The relationship of soul to body is here so different from what you have been accustomed to, that faculties automatically decay when they are employed for a deceptive purpose which the soul inwardly rejects. You sense already in your movement that close dependence of the limbs upon the soul which makes action effortless yet, at the same time, exhilarating. This condition is the direct result of your submission to me, which makes our present rapid progress possible. It is not easy to explain all this scientifically to a beginner: but perhaps you can conceive of a soul acting directly upon bodily faculties in such a way that the sluggishness of the flesh is by-passed."

"Quantum non noxia corpora tardant
Terrenique hebetant artus moribundaque membra."[1]

The lines sang in my head. I was scarcely conscious of uttering them audibly. Perhaps I didn't; but the angel received them.

"Ah yes, you've read Virgil. The word *sluggishness* took you back to construing in the fifth form. Very proper that it should. Though, of course, Virgil didn't mean quite what we mean. It was his especial grace that he said much more than he meant."

I had not yet learned the foolishness of thrusting

[1]As much as earthly limbs, and gross allay
Of mortal members, subject to decay,
Blunt not the beams of heaven and edge of day.
                    Virgil: *Aeneid*, Dryden's Translation.

repartee into angelic discourse, and I made a very silly remark.

"Virgil said more than he meant. Does this mean that I shall find him in the Department for the Dumb?"

"You are not so stupid as to expect me to appear outwitted. I can only assume therefore that you expect me to appear amused. It is one thing to say, by inspiration, more than you mean; and quite another thing to convey, by deceptive intention, more than you feel. This, I suppose, is clear to you. What is not clear to you is the fact that certain jokes make no appeal to angels. Among them are jokes which assume a prevalent tendency to verbal confusion."

I felt sufficiently flattened by this rebuke. I also felt that there was something of unfriendly detachment, if not of actual hostility, in the angel's attitude. Why should he thus trouble to break a butterfly on a wheel? What did it matter? Were we engaged upon something so utterly momentous that all casual conversation must be subjected to the devastating analysis of a *viva voce* examination? For the first time, I began to feel tired, and to ask myself where we were going. The pace was quick. Why should it be? And in an instant a great weariness seized upon me, so that my legs struggled laboriously, my chest heaved, and I panted aloud.

"Ah," said the angel, "you wonder where we are going."

What a stupid thing to say, I thought, and a sudden cramp shot through my legs. My hand dragged at his. I stumbled and spluttered. Where were we going? What was the use? And, with a lurch, I fell flat on the ground.

"Worse and worse. You not only wonder where we are going. You even question whether it is worthwhile to go there. And this is the result."

"Or perhaps the cause," I gasped. I was flat out, but determined not to give in. This seemed to be the aptest way of expressing my annoyance.

"Cause or result," he murmured placidly. "Yes, that too is a relationship which we must explore. But not yet; except in so far as this particular predicament requires elucidation. What did I tell you a moment ago about the connection between our rapid progress and your temporary submission to my guardianship? You questioned where we were going, and it was a weariness to your limbs. You doubted whether you wanted to go there, and it was nothing less than the exhaustion of your whole frame. Though it is true that your vitality flickered out in one last stinging rebuke—ill-directed as it happened. Perhaps, if your rebuke had been directed otherwhere—to yourself and not to me—the result might have been different...or the cause: what you will."

I knew when I was beaten, and it was inglorious to lick the dust.

"No," I said, and the breath came more easily, "not what *I* will: that isn't getting me anywhere. What *you* will. Nothing else is of use to me here."

He lifted me to my feet and spoke again, but without coldness.

"What *I* will? That is your way of putting it. Perhaps you too mean more than you say."

I knew at once; and at once I was refreshed.

"Of course," I said, "of course. What *He* wills."

And, with a majestic bound, we were in flight again.

2

"Joe Crosset, you can rest assured that you were quite wrong to leave your wife, even under that provocation; but there is no cause to talk about that kind of thing here. We are not examining your moral life. All we have to do in this court is to find a means of keeping you occupied. The rest will come later. Now, what trade did you follow?"

The speaker, a venerable angel of majestic dimensions, sat in the centre of a dais, unencumbered by table, book or pen, whilst lesser angelic figures busied themselves with books and writing at his side. These sat at long tables, arranged on either side so that they could command a view both of their President and of those he addressed. Just now the President leaned forward towards a wrinkled, lean-faced old man with a pointed nose and keen, but bewildered eyes. On earth he would have looked tall.

"I am a stonemason, sir." He instinctively turned forwards the palms of his hands as he spoke, and looked down at them, half-fondly, half-pityingly.

"Excellent. It is most fortunate for you that you have been trained to such useful work. We receive so many people nowadays with untrained hands and un-sharpened brains, and it is often most difficult to oc-cupy them. You, Joe, can be set to work without delay. Ruziel, conduct him to the Office of Works."

The old man shuffled awkwardly as Ruziel ap-proached, and he cast a furtive glance of fear at the President, before turning to leave the presence. The President gravely inclined his head as Joe Crosset turned, and the interview was over. Joe passed beside us where we sat at the bottom of the long hall, remote from the dais, shadowed and sheltered by the massive pillars which rose into dim arches high above us. It did not strike me as odd that I could clearly hear the quiet talk from the distant dais, nor that I could clearly see the expressions on the far faces of the angels who sat there; yet I think now that it was this remark-able proximity in distance which awed us into stillness and silence as we sat, each awaiting his turn to be ex-amined.

"Alexander Wrose!"

As the name rang out, a short, rather flabby indi-vidual, with thick horn-rimmed spectacles clinging to a shiny bald head, rose from amongst us and walked confidently up to the dais. The President kept his eyes upon him as he approached.

"*You* were not a stonemason, I think."

"No, sir. A civil servant."

"Ah yes; clerical work."

"Of a fairly high quality, sir. I made progress. Cleri-cal Assistant at seventeen; Clerical Officer at twenty-four; Executive Officer at thirty-six. I had my own office then. I was only a hundred a year below a car-pet and a whole typist."

"A whole typist?"

"Yes, sir, I never graduated to that; but I was allowed half a typist. She was in my office on Mondays, Wednesdays and Friday mornings. On Tuesdays and Thursdays I had to fetch my own coffee. Single sugar lump, of course. Twelve hundred a year before you get a sugar bowl."

"I see. And did you like your work?"

"I did, sir. Complete security, clean hands, regular increments, and thirty-six days off a year. Add to that Bank Holidays, the Queen's Birthday, Sundays and three days' sick leave. And no need to turn out on Saturday mornings...."

"Yes, but the work—was it congenial?"

"It certainly was, sir. I retired at sixty, with a pension of x/8oths of my average income for the last five years, where x equals the number of pensionable years in the service. In addition there was a gratuity, a lump sum equal to a year's average salary. And I took advantage of the new scheme which allowed me to forfeit half my lump sum in return for a guaranteed pension for the wife in the event of my death. You can appreciate how glad I am now about that. Foresight always pays."

"I asked you about the work you did?"

"Yes, sir, to be sure. It was not every man's meat perhaps, but it suited me down to the ground. A fifteen minutes' ride on the bus, half-an-hour in the tube, and there I was, regular as clockwork. The office was cosy—I'm simple in my tastes, the central heating very reliable, and things ran very smoothly. I always found my newspaper on the desk ready waiting for me."

"My dear fellow, it's the work I'm interested in. Tell

me something about that. Answer a plain question. Did you find it dull?"

"Lord bless you, no, sir. Why, the window over-looked a busy street. There was always something going on. Besides, I had a telephone. I could ring up my wife at any time. Very comforting. I always rang back home sharp on ten o'clock. Susie isn't what you'd call a nervous woman, but she liked to know that I was safe and sound. Such terrible things happen these days. You never know. What with cosh boys and train smashes, a man takes his life into his hands every time he travels to work."

The President sighed and raised his hand.

"But work, my dear Alexander, is the very thing you refuse to talk about; and it happens to be the thing we are particularly interested in. You will force me to conclude that it played no part in your daily cycle. What did your employers require you to do in this office?"

"My special line was checking up on subsections 7c and 7d of 321/HHJ/77's, but a fair number of PX/594's came my way too. We filed the details in triplicate. Of course I had a regular flow of minutes from above to initial, and of chits from below to sign. And I dictated replies to letters of enquiry. Another two-fifty a year, sir, and I should have been able to dictate completely original letters that were not replies to anything at all."

"Alexander, you make it extremely difficult for us to place you properly. Tell me; did you initiate anything? Did you have to make decisions?"

"Oh, no, sir. Decisions never come from anybody under two thousand a year. That's the Indian-carpet-and-two-armchairs level. I didn't get anywhere near that. I had the wrong sort of schooling."

"You needn't tell us more about that. It is clear to me that your work has not equipped you for positive service up here. Perhaps you had a hobby. You gardened?"

"I mowed the lawn on Sundays, sir, in summer; but I didn't like digging and that kind of thing."

"You read, perhaps?"

"Only the daily paper, sir, and *John Bull* at the weekends. I was always too tired to concentrate in the evenings."

"Then how did you pass your time?"

"Listening to the radio mostly, sir. We were both very fond of the Quiz programmes and *Twenty Questions*. They keep you alert and up-to-date."

The President shook his head in grave disappointment.

"I am afraid, Alexander, that I shall have to register you as temporarily unoccupiable. I'm sorry. Though I have reason to doubt whether you will find complete vacuity a strain—at least, for a time. I regret that we cannot provide you with a radio. You were happiest with that, I gather."

"Oh, yes, sir. I could sit for hours listening to it, smoking my pipe..."

The President's eyes lit up.

"Smoking your pipe! Ah; you smoked and enjoyed it?"

"I did, sir."

"Splendid. You appreciate a smoke-laden atmosphere?"

"Perfectly at home in it, sir."

"And you can puff with restrained and solemn regularity?"

"Certainly, sir."

"It is a great relief. I was on the point of dismissing you as a wholly negative case. Ruziel, conduct Alexander to the Training Department for Thurifers."

The examination of Alexander Wrose had caused a certain amount of discomfiture among us who waited. One or two individuals had shifted uneasily in their seats whilst listening to the dialogue, and an audible sigh of relief emanated from several throats when the next name rang out down the hall.

"Henry St. John Riddiough!"

We watched the square shoulders and erect head of a brisk, well-built figure gliding smoothly up the hall. The back, at least, spoke of confidence and urbanity. The President gazed intently as before; and there was a slight pause before he spoke.

"You will realize now, Henry, what it is that we wish to know. You filled some useful role on earth, I'm sure. Tell me something of your qualifications."

"Carchester and Old College."

"That doesn't tell me much about you, Henry."

"It's a label of some consequence in some quarters, sir." Riddiough glanced knowingly at the other angels on the dais. "I have no doubt there are Carcastrians among you. Perhaps you will grant your colleagues the opportunity to lay their cards on the table. I should spot the Carcastrian touch somewhere, I've no doubt. With your permission, I'll put a few exploratory questions to them."

"I'm sorry to disappoint you," said the President firmly, "but it is your business to answer questions; ours to ask them."

"A pity you take it like that. It's not quite the code I

looked for. You'd find the team serving you the better, if you gave them each a turn in the nets. And I'd appreciate the chance to try them out. A man likes to know his friends."

"We are all your friends, Henry; though we have perhaps been bred to a rather different tradition. You did well at school?"

"Not a bookworm, sir; but Snippett, my house-master, thought very highly of me. Powers of leadership, you know, and that kind of thing. And Snippett was in a position to judge: he knew me best of anyone. Prepared me for confirmation, if that's relevant—I believe it's rather in your line. Not that Snippett was a believer, of course. They always try to avoid that kind of bias at Carchester."

"It would help me to fit you into a suitable occupation here, if you could give me some account of your special talents." The President spoke gently but with an air of persistence, as if implying that an answer of some kind would have to be found. "You would account yourself a person of distinctive talents?"

"I made my mark in the right circles; but a fellow does not care to advertise himself in public."

"Plain facts we are asking for, Henry, not self-advertisement. In what subjects did you excel whilst at school?"

"I didn't exactly hit the headlines as a scholar. My family wouldn't have wished it. We have never gone in for that kind of thing."

"And your university career?"

"Very stimulating. It gave the article the right finishing touch. There's a great deal to be said for the Varsity; it teaches one to mix—and one is old enough to know where to draw the line."

"You attained some academic distinction?"

"Not my line, as I've said before. Couldn't make Honour Mods. And I must say that the fellows who burrowed in libraries missed a great deal."

"Then for what kind of work are you equipped, Henry?"

"Any work of responsibility, sir; anything that calls for leadership and the exercise of authority."

"But over what specific sphere of activity can you claim a right to exercise responsibility? Whither are you qualified to lead? Wherein lies your authority?"

"If I may say so, these are petty questions. I find this minute interest in qualifications positively vulgar. I was not trained to menial or professional tasks. I was educated for leadership. You drive me to a most disagreeable pose of self-display. I regret it, even as I adopt it. No man ought to have to dilate upon his own abilities. Let me be placed where initiative can be exercised and commands given."

"By whom?"

Riddiough drew himself up to his full height and gave an unflinching reply.

"By those most fitted to assert themselves over their fellow men."

"Henry!" The President's shout came like a clap of thunder. "There are utterances which even now can sweep you from our midst. Think seriously before you speak. Try to understand your present position, even if it bears no resemblance to anything in your past experience. Let me explain your situation. You stand here divested of all authority. You now dwell in a sphere where your capacity for leadership, such as it is, must remain inoperative. In such a situation, have you anything to contribute to the life of the community?"

"Such a preposterous situation, sir, renders my whole education valueless."

"Exactly."

"It throws doubt upon the principles of the tradition in which I was bred."

"It does."

"Then I may say that you speak unadvisedly. I have been purposely misunderstood. But you are yourself responsible to higher authorities, and I am confident that among those higher authorities I shall find Carcastrians in key positions. It is unthinkable that it should be otherwise. When my case comes before them, I shall no doubt be given my proper place at their side. You will then be privileged to see a display of tolerance—the tolerance of a gentleman in authority towards those subordinates who have injured him."

I have never heard a silence more profound than that which followed these words. The secretarial angels had one and all ceased to write, and each one sat with lowered head, pen laid aside and hands resting, palms downwards, on his book. The President's head remained upright, but his eyes were closed. Riddiough stood motionless and, far away at the bottom of the hall, we held our breath and kept our eyes fixed upon his formidable back. At length the President opened his eyes and spoke.

"Ruziel!"

The angel came forward from the great doors behind us. At that moment one of the angelic secretaries raised his head and seized his book, as if about to tear out a page. The President caught his movement and raised his hand.

"No," he said, "it is not as bad as that. A near thing,

though. You will come here again, Henry. At least, I hope so. The Special School, Ruziel."

We did not know whether to admire or pity the Carcastrian as he strode past us, still erect, and left the hall. Nor could we yet share the relaxation of tension which was plainly felt by the angelic figures on the dais. Glimpses of wrath in the last examination had further unnerved us, and I for one did not know which I wished the more ardently to avoid—instant examination or a further period of suspense. But it was not my turn yet. The name "Ian Brew" was called, and a debonair, silver-headed man, with a neat moustache, regular features and lively eyes, presented himself for examination. The President eyed him more curiously than his predecessors, and bade him be at ease.

"I can no longer be at ease," said Brew excitedly. "Frankly, I've had enough of this now, and I shall be glad when I wake up. I don't mind what you do, so long as it shocks me back to consciousness. Ring a bell, or something: then perhaps I shall grab the telephone receiver, and come round in the surgery armchair, or in bed—I can't remember where I was when I fell asleep."

"You think you're dreaming," said the President slowly.

"What else? A little more vividly than usual. That's the toasted cheese, no doubt. But I've had enough of it."

For the first time, the President turned aside and formally addressed his colleagues on the dais.

"This is too bad. The duties of this tribunal have been quite clearly defined, and look what happens.

We have neither the time nor the equipment to deal here with this kind of case. He should have been sent straight away to the Psycho-therapeutic Department, where they have everything on hand for treating cases of Traumatic-fantasy. As I have said before, the new organization is not above criticism. Before the fashion for departmentalization set in, we were able, in each court, to take a proper survey of freshmen from every point of view. Now, when we have been confined officially to what can only be called glorified talent-spotting, we find ourselves landed time after time with candidates requiring preliminary treatment which can only be given elsewhere. Too much responsibility is being placed upon Guardian Angels. They have to make a quick selection of the appropriate court for the first examination of freshmen. And yet, by the very nature of their regular duties and preoccupations, many Guardians are imperfectly informed about the departmental organization."

The President's speech was interrupted by the candidate himself, whose excitement seemed to have increased immeasurably.

"You're quite right. An overorganized administration is the very devil, if you don't mind my saying so. I ought to know. I'm a G.P. I can understand your feelings and sympathize with them. There was a time when I was able to consider a patient as a man, sick in body, or perhaps in mind, and requiring a personal sort of consideration which took everything into account. Centralized administration has altered all that. The human patient has been organized out of existence. I have to deal instead with a candidate for this specialized treatment or else for that. The poor fellow has got to be labelled and despatched to some department which understands only one germ, one organ or one limb."

The President, who had turned again to face his examinee, was visibly cheered.

"Ian, my friend, you speak quite sensibly. What a pity it is that you're asleep."

"Oh, yes," said the doctor, as if recollecting himself suddenly, "I'd almost forgotten."

"You'd quite forgotten, I think. Or perhaps you've changed your mind."

"No. I'm not continuously aware of being asleep, of course. It would be an even more ridiculous dream if I were. But when I stop to reflect, I realize that sooner or later I must wake up."

"That makes communication between us very difficult, since I am undoubtedly awake."

The doctor laughed and began to muse aloud.

"It is very odd. One can be fitfully aware in a dream of being asleep. That's common enough. It's a kind of anchorage which often keeps one from being utterly overwhelmed during a nightmare. But to sustain, in a dream, a conversation upon the question whether one is dreaming—that is very odd; so odd that it warrants a paper in one of the journals. I must write it up."

The President looked at the doctor intently.

"You have not even now fully measured the oddity of the situation. The dream not only allows you to conduct an argument upon the question whether you are dreaming: it also allows you to reflect upon yourself as being involved in that argument, and to visualize yourself as commenting upon that complex state of consciousness at some future date. And now, as you listen to me, a new detachment, a further level of awareness is added. You picture yourself as reflecting upon yourself as being involved in the argument whether you..."

"Stop, please stop. I've grasped your point, of course. It renders the experience so complex that——"

"It is useless for literary purposes."

"I wonder."

"Come now, doctor. On what do you base your assumption that this is a dream?"

"Simply on the fact that I just don't believe in this kind of thing at all."

"Quite so. You don't believe in it. And yet you have been brought to this Department as though you did believe in *some* kind of way—as though there were some inner direction of the will towards belief. For I may as well tell you that you would not have appeared before this tribunal, had it not been assumed that you shaped your life in the fashion of a believer. I can explain this to you. For it is no mystery to me. I have too much experience of Selection Boards to be in doubt. It is all due to the inveterate tenderness of the Guardians towards certain members of your profession. No, it is not your knowledge they respect; still less your professional status; nor your achievements in healing, which are, of course, not strictly *your* achievements at all. The Guardians are touched by your obedience. They see you live your lives through at the beck and call of others. They see you rise in the night and set out, not because you *know* the case warrants it, but because a certain code just has to be obeyed. Obedience is very near to faith: indeed, it is the nearest thing to faith. The Guardians have the scope of life continually under survey. They find this spectacle of obedience a very distinctive thing in your century. They allow it to blind them to questions which are, frankly, even more important. Well, you have to take Guardians as you find them; and this tenderness towards obedient men is one of their notorious weaknesses."

"I can't for the life of me understand," said the doctor, "why they should set such store by mechanical obedience of that kind."

"Why should you expect to understand anything at all, if you are not in full command of your faculties? Well, I will answer your question nevertheless. Obedience is never mechanical: it never can be mechanical. Obedience is wilful submission to an external command. If it is not wilful, it is not obedience. No machine can act wilfully: therefore no machine can obey. 'Mechanical obedience' is thus a nonsensical contradiction in terms. Obedience is a specifically human virtue."

"You are not a creature to argue with," said the doctor, "for that is a good debating point. So good that I shall have to drop the word 'mechanical': but I still maintain that the kind of behaviour on my part which has apparently endeared me to these creatures whom you call Guardians—I still maintain that this kind of behaviour detracts from the dignity of human beings. Jumping out of bed at the sound of a bell, I mean, and rushing off into the night without any real assurance that such urgent measures are necessary. In point of fact, they are quite unnecessary in the vast majority of cases. That is why I maintain that it ought to go against the grain with any self-respecting human being. Mechanical or not, I never feel less like a man nor more like a machine, than when I answer the night bell."

"The old-fashioned educationalists are quite right,"

said the President. "You medical men suffer enormously from deficiencies in linguistic and logical training. *Of course* that kind of behaviour goes against the grain; that is why it requires a special exercise of the will; and that is why it is utterly unmechanical and utterly human. I'm afraid you cannot shake yourself free of your few really virtuous actions by the pleas that you didn't enjoy performing them. You only magnify the virtues by these disclaimers. And that is rather bad form, don't you think?"

The doctor laughed heartily.

"That I should stand here and be publicly accused of notorious virtues is odd enough—but no odder than the rest of this incredible fantasy. However, you make it quite clear that there is no effective defence against the charge. I must be content with a salvation unwittingly—but wilfully—procured."

"Oh, please don't imagine that *that* is at stake here and now. We are merely concerned with your occupation. The irregularities in your case and your own persistence have led me to make excursions into matters which, strictly speaking, lie outside my official province here. One irregularity leads to another in the administrative world. You were brought before me and it is right that I should deal with you. Since you plead guilty to the charge of continual obedience, I shall sentence you to a period of menial servitude. This occupation will give play to your distinctive talent; and it will sure cure you of feeling asleep. Menial Servitude, Ruziel."

There was no pause before the next name was called—"Harriett Templecombe"—and a dignified lady in the fifties swept majestically, if fussily, up to the dais.

"I am delighted to meet you," she exclaimed, seizing the initiative. "I may say that I have been most impressed by your manner of conducting this assembly. It is not everyone who has the right touch for this kind of thing, as I well know. Indeed, if efficient chairmen had been easier to come by, my own life would have been a great deal easier. I should have been freed from many burdensome demands upon my time and patience. But I never spared myself—and I know what costly work this chairmanship is. I know what it takes out of you. I know the nervous strain which the chairman's placid demeanour so often conceals. It is courageous work. I commend you all the more for your delicacy in handling the examinees. I was so afraid there might be unseemliness—too much candour in self-expression, you know. I have met that kind of thing among the Buchmanites. But your guiding hand unobtrusively preserves the tone. The tone is so important, isn't it, in a gathering like this—so easily lowered, so hardly sustained. And your tolerance is an example to all. 'There will be no dogmatism in Heaven.' How often I have heard my husband, the Archdeacon, say that! And how right he was. But of course you have seen him already, and admired him, I'm sure. When shall I meet him?"

The question brought a pause to the rapid flow of words; and the President was at last able to speak.

"If I remember rightly, your husband is in the Backward Believers' Department."

"Oh, no, no. There must be some mistake. My husband was in orders—Archdeacon Templecombe. He wrote a book called *Crisis for Christianity: a study in reconciling the Faith to Modern Thought.*"

"Yes, that *was* the trouble, I believe."

But the reply was unheeded, and the words flowed again.

"It was acclaimed by the reviewers and won almost universal approval. 'A courageous blow at sectarianism and obscurantism'—that was the kind of thing they said; and it warmed my dear husband's heart. 'It cuts like a clean knife through the nets of archaic dogma and unscrutinized superstition'—I shall always remember that. The publisher printed it on the dust flap of the second edition. You see, my husband was never content that the Church should stand still. 'The Church must move with the times, it must unbend,' he used to say. 'The Church must return to the people.' I think that's so right, so Christian, don't you?"

"We are not examining your husband, Harriett."

"No, no, of course not. How foolish of me. You know him perfectly well already. You have learned to admire him and to imitate him—I can see that. You are so understanding, so sympathetic. His spirit has infected you; and you have learned that we are all members of one big family. How glad I am that he came where he was most needed. It was my comfort, when he left me, to realize that God needed him even more than I did. And I see now in your humane bearing that my husband's work has left its mark here already. He has taught you too to unbend. I knew he would. Sometimes, when he was attacked by bigots for his broadmindedness and tolerance, he would say to me, 'Harriett, I can't be other than I am. I can't be other than God made me. I must be myself. It is my mission to humanize the Church. And if, by God's will, I were to be transferred to Heaven tomorrow, I should start straight away to humanize Heaven.' He has done so. And all we who come after share the benefit of his great work—a humanized Heaven. He has let you into the secret of his humility.... No, no, you mustn't mind what I say. I must speak my mind. 'Be sincere, Harriett,' my husband used to say. 'Be sincere: it is better to sin sincerely than to be hypocritically pious.' That was humble, wasn't it?"

The President lifted his hand for a pause, and leaned forward, as if to ensure attention.

"You are not giving us the information we want, Harriett."

"How foolish of me. I chatter away, don't I? That's because I feel so at home. I feel as though I've known you all my life. As indeed I have. You've been at my side: I know it. Angel voices ever singing. I've heard you and known you always in that deep spiritual way. That is why I'm so at home now. I knew that you would be real persons—not standing stiffly, with crowns in your hands, around a crystal sea—but just like this, real *human* angels....Oh, yes, I'm sorry. You want me to tell you about my work. It was a great mission, but I did not falter. I did my very best to support my husband in his labours for the kingdom. A woman can be such a great help to a true minister, can't she?—the right sort of woman, I mean. I lifted the whole burden of our social life from my husband's shoulders. There were so many people to meet, so many people to entertain. Churchwardens could be dealt with over morning coffee, and Mothers' Union secretaries were honoured to be invited to tea; but canons and rural deans had to be asked to lunch, and the Bishop, of course, to dinner. I had my problems with the servants, but I kept them to myself. I believe there never was a more unflurried hostess, even when cook was working without a kitchen-maid."

"You have no children, I believe?"

"I had to deny myself that happiness. My husband sometimes expressed a wish for a son. But I'm sure I was right. It would have been selfish to give myself to family affairs, when his position made such demands upon me in the social sphere. It was his well-being that I had at heart always. I could not have endured to see his work suffer and to be myself the cause. Our social commitments made it quite impossible for me to think of rearing a family. I have seen the wives of clergy—even of canons residentiary—obsessed with their numerous children, whilst their husbands were fretted with domestic cares. The husbands suffered in consequence. They had no social background. It did them no good. And it did no good to the Church. These things get talked about."

"It is clear that a great many things get talked about, Harriett, but the facts relevant to this tribunal are unfortunately not among them. I gather that you have no experience of children and no personal experience of domestic work."

"No, no. I gave myself without stint to the support of my husband and his labours. I sat on dozens of commitees. The Mothers' Union claimed a great deal of my time. And I presided over the Diocesan Committee for Moral Welfare. A woman's knowledge and experience are invaluable for directing work of that kind, don't you think? Then there was the Diocesan Education Committee: I was always most attentive to that. Where the future generation is concerned, the voice of up-to-date Churchmanship has just got to be heard. I was much in demand too as a public speaker. I think I gave my address, 'Preparing for Christian Wifehood,' to every branch of the Girls' Friendly Society in the diocese."

"And you bore no children."

"My work would have been impossible had I not denied myself that happiness. I was always at the service of the Church societies. After all, as my husband used to say, it is in the societies that one really sees the Church at work. There the Church lives. It was an inspiration to hear my husband counter the charge that Church attendances were falling off. 'We must not measure our achievement by the fact that formal acts of public worship do not appeal to the modern mind,' he used to say. 'There is something distinctly healthy in the refusal of the younger generation to accept conventions unquestioningly. They express themselves in new ways through the social activities of the modern Church. At heart they are deeply religious; but they suspect hypocrisy and detest empty conventions. Let their act of worship be an evening of good fellowship in the bright warm clubroom, instead of a mechanical flow of words in a dim, cold church. It is not the less acceptable to God for that.' "

"I do not think, Harriett, that at this stage we can usefully consider the question what things are most agreeable to God. I have the impression that it will be some time before you and I will be equally qualified to discuss that matter. If you will keep silent for a few moments, I will try to make clear what your present situation is. Let me explain that, generally speaking, we find women much easier to deal with than men. Most women have experience of dealing with children or doing household tasks, which makes it a simple matter to occupy them usefully here. You, however, are an exception. There are no committees to which you could contribute anything. There are no social occasions over which you would be qualified to preside. Were you ever involved in any activity at all in which you did not discuss, direct, speak or preside?—Any activity in which you actually *did* something?"

"I led prayers at..."

"No, no. That won't do."

"I adjudicated..."

"Sorry. Not what we want."

"I organized..."

"I'm afraid your mind is running in the wrong direction. I can see little hope. Did you not, perhaps as a girl in school, play a part in some distinct and positive corporate effort?"

"I sang in the school choir."

"Splendid."

"I'm afraid not. It was a failure. I had no ear for music. I found myself quite unfitted for leadership in that sphere; so naturally I dropped it."

"Admirable. That is really something to build upon. You shall be thoroughly trained. Ruziel, see that she is taken to the Choir School."

These were the last words I heard before the blow fell. For a moment later I heard my own name called, and suspense gave way suddenly—not to despair—but to a kind of calm expectancy. I cannot explain this. I had expected that, when my turn came, I should be smitten with a feverish dread. I had pictured myself dragging trembling legs up the hall, with that absurd lack of control over my lower limbs which has always marked the crises in my worst nightmares. I had feared lest I might collapse before the dais, and I had watched the confidence of my predecessors there with astonishment and envy. Now I began to realize that a part, at least, of their confidence had not been derived from within. For I felt myself drawn firmly and calmly towards the dais by a power not my own. As I took my station before the President, I was conscious of an enveloping support which made standing as restful as sitting.

The President looked a little disappointed as he studied me.

"One stonemason to four people who have never learned to use their hands. This is not a fruitful session."

I suddenly felt horribly useless. Automatically my untrained hands slid behind my back.

"Were you too a civil servant?"

I had always flattered myself that I couldn't be mistaken for one. Perhaps there were similarities that I had overlooked.

"No, sir," I said. "I was a teacher."

"Ah, yes. A peculiarly useless qualification up here, where there is nothing that you can teach and everything for you to learn."

"I always continued to study, sir."

"Of course you did. Chiefly in order to make your teaching the more impressive. The learning was a mere personal equipment. You didn't really want to know: you merely wanted to be known as one who knew. Not my province to press that home; but you ought to understand why it is that we must seek for some more solid activity—though I doubt whether we shall find anything."

My thoughts went back to the civil servant. He had been let down easily, I felt. I ventured to claim an affinity.

"Well, sir, I too smoke a pipe."

"It won't do, I'm afraid. Alexander Wrose smoked for the sheer pleasure of it. You used tobacco as a drug to assist study."

I admitted that it was so.

"That, I believe, was your excuse for not giving it up in Lent. No tobacco, no study. The idea has now been introduced by the Underworld to the clergy. No tobacco, no sermons. What hobby did you cultivate?"

"I wrote books, sir."

"Of what kind?"

I had been purposely vague, hoping that this question would not come. Indeed I cherished the expectation that my work had become known above. To be honest, this idea was a kind of compensation for my comparative failure down below, where sales were miserably small. Surely up here they watched the life of the Church: surely they knew who were Her defenders on earth, however humble. I feared the President was trying to trap me into boasting.

"Of what kind?"

The question was repeated with an air of deliberate admonition that could not be ignored. I spoke with a tremble.

"They were all informed with Christian principles, sir, and might count as a kind of apologetic."

"Ah, yes. And what can we do here, do you think, with a qualification of that kind? Does it not strike you that there is little scope here for the art of proving the existence of God? Can you see any good reason why you should not join Archdeacon Templecombe in the Backward Believers' Department?"

I could see a dozen good reasons why I shouldn't. But was it prudent to mention them? Should I not be self-condemned for vanity and arrogance? I remembered my Guardian's advice, however, and spoke my mind briefly.

"I do not think, sir, that I could be accused of teaching a diluted Christianity."

"Exactly. You could not be accused of teaching it. But perhaps you could be accused of practising it?"

I was silent.

"Come, now," said the President. "We must face the facts. You were one of those people who *knew* that the Faith is a religion. No virtue of yours, that. A given intellectual insight. You happened to come across one or two good instructors in your youth. The point is— what did you do about it? The answer is simple. You went about explaining to others that the Faith is a religion, and nothing else. A convenient solution to your dilemma. You enjoyed the satisfaction of knowing that you were speaking the truth; whilst absolving yourself from any kind of obligation to act upon it. There are ugly words to describe this sort of thing. You yourself have a good store of them; and you distributed them pretty generously in your day. I think you had an ingenious way of pushing off the personal challenge when it came too near. 'Some are called to minister, some to labour, some to teach.' A question of individual vocation. And *you* were called to teach. It saved a lot of trouble, didn't it?"

I was quite unable to reply and, after a frightening pause, the President proceeded.

"We have a school for Advanced Gnostics. You will not misunderstand the use of the word *advanced*. It is in Gnosticism that these people are far advanced. But few perhaps so far advanced as yourself, who have spent your days attacking Gnosticism. What more ingenious than your intellectual attack upon the view that the Faith can be fully explored at the intellectual level? Do you not think this sufficient reason for me to commit you to the College for Gnostics?"

"I shouldn't have chosen the place," I said.

"An evasive answer; though it would be illuminating to know what you would choose for yourself. I think I will give you the opportunity of stating a preference. It is plain that you can occupy yourself properly only in an educational institution. You shall see what the provisions are. Ruziel, arrange for his Guardian to take him to visit both the College for Gnostics at Helicon and the Backward Believers' Department at Fordshaw. I will re-examine him later."

On that inauspicious note my examination ended.

3

"You were disappointed in the Selection Tribunal?"

I looked up from my musing to see the welcome face of my Guardian, Lamiel. Ruziel had told me his name, and had assured me that I should soon meet him again, which somewhat lessened my surprise now. I rose hastily and bowed, but he bade me be seated again.

"You have found a very pleasant seat."

It was a flat slab of rock embedded in the ground at the foot of a giant fir tree. Before me, as I sat there, the ground swept down, thick with bracken, to a swift stream which was largely hidden by the huge boulders lying in its bed. Here and there conifers studded the steep banks on either side, so that the ground was sprinkled with patches of light and shade; for the sun was behind us. It was what I should have called a winter sunlight; for the trees and rocks and foliage stood out with an almost frosty clarity: but I did not feel cold, and there was in fact nothing to suggest winter in what I actually saw. Here was the greenery of spring seen in the bare light of a January sun. Lamiel spoke again as I reseated myself.

"You were musing when I interrupted you—probably about your first experience of our more formal proceedings."

"Yes," I said, for I had several times runover in my mind the strange sequence of examinations. "What I cannot properly understand is this. Why should an examination so grave in appearance lead to such trivial conclusions?"

"Is it trivial to build walls or to burn incense in worship?"

"No, it isn't. I didn't mean that. But all these people—all we freshmen, that is—we have such a lot to learn, and such a lot to unlearn, I daresay; yet no opportunity seems to be offered to begin to put things right. Perhaps we *began* on earth, just a little, to understand what things are really important and what things deserve far less attention than we gave to them; but it is back to these less deserving activities that we are directed. Take my own case: if I have to get away from thinking and talking to actual doing, oughtn't I to be set to some practical discipline straight away?"

"So that you may have a new acquisition to flatter yourself about?" Lamiel smiled gravely.

"Well, there's a risk, I admit. But I can't get anywhere by going back to the old pursuits. Surely an educational institution is the last place for me. And the stonemason; hasn't he built enough walls for one man? Isn't there a side of his nature which was quite undeveloped on earth, and which it would be rich for him to develop now?"

"You would rather see him start on the study of logic, theology or music?"

"Yes, I would. That's how I pictured things here."

"Whilst you, who were not skilled enough to knock

up a tolerable garden wall on earth, should be allowed to try your hand at botched-up building in Heaven. Is that what you mean?"

"I should have to learn, I know that. But wouldn't it do me good?"

"Maybe it would, in a sense, but it would also leave Heaven littered with jerry-built walls. I won't labour the question whether you ought to regard this community you have entered as being primarily designed to benefit you. Ought you, in any case, to advocate a general holiday for everybody from their accustomed tasks? A grand Vacation Summer School, in which everybody applied themselves to the cultivation of leisure-time pursuits, might create a universal holiday spirit. I doubt whether it would provide the disciplines required here."

"But surely I need to learn to do things, and the stonemason needs to learn to think."

I turned to look up at Lamiel, as he stood there behind me, erect against the trunk of the tree. He nodded his head, as if in acquiescence, but his voice had a distant tone.

"You might both have profited at one time from an interchange of occupations; that is true enough. But I deprecate the presupposition that our Hierarchies exist to compensate you here and now for opportunities of this kind neglected below. The Cherubim and Seraphim would not be happy to find themselves regarded as the administrative centre of a superlunary W.E.A."

I began to feel annoyed. Lamiel was plainly making fun of me. He was twisting my words so as to distort my real meaning. I countered him hastily and with a touch of irritation.

"No, no. I am not asking that everyone should learn

a new job, just because the job is different and therefore interesting. That is not my meaning at all. I ask
merely that we should begin to move in the right direction. Even on earth we saw men with vastly richer
lives than our own—men on the road to sanctity,
marked out by their good works and their piety, some
even by their apprehension down below of what is
here in store for them. Isn't this a road which we must
all travel? And isn't it time that we made a start?"

"It is indeed. But do you think you can leap into the
practice of sanctity like a man diving into a swimming
pool? Do you imagine that you have merely to strip off
the trappings of earthly interests in order to be pure
and clean for bathing in the waters of Divine Love?
You wish to outgrow these earthly interests. Well and
good. But does it not occur to you that, if you were
suddenly divested of them, there might be nothing
left? You speak foolishly and you speak in irritation,
and you justly deserve rebuke. Be content to listen,
and perhaps things will be made plain to you."

I leaned forward in shame, though the rebuke was
largely beyond my understanding.

"I'm sorry," I said. "I was thinking aloud. My statements were questions really. Of course I want to be
put right where I am wrong."

"That is generous of you," said the angel, with his
strange quality of irony, which cut without bitterness
and made the wound seem like the gift of a friend.
"Your error is to imagine that you can go straight out
for the things you want—or need—and get them. You
cannot. You are a human being. It is a part of your
very nature that the things most requisite for your
happiness, health and salvation, should be attained
only as by-products and never as directly pursued

ends. The very condition of finitude, in which you have been reared, ensures this. If a man wishes his family to be happy, does he stay at home to romp and joke all day with his children and to fondle his wife? Of course not. He goes out to work and make money, so that he can provide his family with the necessities of life and as much more as possible. Is the healthy man the man who makes health the sole object of all his daily activities? Of course not. The healthy man is the man who walks because he loves the country and who plays games because he likes sport. You were a teacher: did you teach history to children in the hope of turning them all into historians? Surely this question shows you how absurd your view is. Mere technical equipments can be acquired by exclusive concentration upon particular techniques. A man learns to play the violin by practising it; he learns to box or fence by making these arts the object of his most earnest endeavours. But you do not attain to wisdom by thinking about wisdom, nor to happiness by thinking about happiness. Nor can you attain to health or sanctity thus. No man ever achieved sanctity by the exclusive pursuit of his own soul's well-being. It may be milking cows and feeding hens and paying bills regularly that makes a man wise. It may be ministering to lepers that makes a man healthy and seeking out thieves and harlots that makes a man a saint. In lesser matters than this you have learned that specialization can distort the personality. Would you go to a dypsomaniac for advice about wines? Was there ever a mannequin who knew how to wear comfortable, usable clothes?"

I saw immediately what Lamiel meant. There was no doubt that he was right. The stupidity of my complaint was now quite clear. Indeed I began to wonder whether perhaps my change of state had not dulled my faculties, instead of sharpening them. For surely this was not a mistake I should have made on earth. Often I had smiled at those pathetic small advertisements in the press—"Congenial middle-aged companion required by lady of moderate means." How could anyone expect to find a congenial companion by advertising for congeniality? Search for friendship and sympathy, and you will never find it; but seek out a man with a passion for foreign stamps, butterflies, ballet—or whatever your private enthusiasm is—and, ten to one, you will find a friend.

"I see," I said apologetically. "Searching directly for sanctity would be like searching directly for friendship. These things don't come to one like that. I suppose that is why, on earth, the Church gives us liturgies to perform, rites to enact and obligations to fulfil."

"These things are indispensable, and partly for the very reason you mention. They enable man, whilst acting at the human level, to add another dimension to his experience. Tell a man to pursue the dimension of the spirit, and you may make a lunatic, a spiritualist or a bewildered cynic. Teach him to adopt certain authorized rites and observances, and you may lead him to spirituality. Now this realm, of course, is not finitude, and we angels are not governed by conditions of this kind. That is our privilege; though sometimes it is a source of sadness. For whenever we receive here men of profound sanctity, who have lived within earth's limitations and yet transcended them, we recognize a peculiarly human glory which we can never taste. These, however, are exceptions, and your case is

entirely different. Though you were rooted by faith
and baptism in this order beyond time, you never allowed the roots to grow, and therefore you are a stran-
ger here. Mere release from the environment of
finitude does not transform the earth-bound soul. You
cannot in one moment shake off the character you
have built elsewhere."

"You have answered one of my questions," I said. "I
can see why Joe Crosset must continue to be a builder
in stone, and why I must continue to be a student. But
why should Wrose turn thurifer and Mrs. Templecombe learn to sing? Are not these activities irrelevant?"

Lamiel smiled indulgently.

"You improve a little. 'Irrelevant' is better. I thought
you were going to say 'trivial.' But it still isn't good
enough. Why are those tasks irrelevant?"

"Because they don't seem to connect with the past
experience of Wrose and Mrs. Templecombe. Surely
there was something to build upon in the interests
which these two had on earth."

"You are most inconsistent. First you complain because the tribunal didn't set you and Crosset to something new. Now you complain because Wrose and
Mrs. Templecombe were set to tasks of a kind quite
new to them. Perhaps it will occur to you eventually
that your notion of 'newness' introduces a red-herring
into this discussion. I have told you before, I think,
that you are a child of your time. You have got a bee in
your bonnet about progress. You imagine that our
business is to push you in a certain direction. It isn't.
Our business is simply to turn you inside out. Creatures who have grown accustomed to turn all their experience in upon themselves, perverting objects

worthy of love, worship and enjoyment to the service of their own egos, have got to learn to turn their wills outward in devotion to what is other. The means we use to encourage this reversal vary. You must leave us to judge of their fitness. But do not deceive yourself that you have a journey to go. If you do, you will be tempted to bolster yourself and brace yourself and equip yourself for the enterprise. Here there is no journey. For the self that aspires to a goal, the self that would set out, in determination and in ambitious perseverance—that self has got to be destroyed. If you must image the demand upon you, remember that you are to be turned inside out. We hope that Wrose will learn to delight in incense. And you—if you ever seriously study here—we hope that you will learn to delight in what you study. You will find that a pleasant change from delighting in yourself studying it....But it seems that you are not the only newcomer to discover this quiet valley."

I looked up, as Lamiel's tone changed. Across the valley could be seen two figures, threading their way down the bank towards the stream. One of the two was a man, the other a woman; and I soon recognized the woman as Mrs. Templecombe, the wife of the archdeacon.

"They are both known to you," said Lamiel.

"Are they?" I said in surprise, having recognized only the one. And then, as the two figures reached the stream and stared up at the bank on which we were sitting, I saw that Lamiel was right. For the man's face brought back memories of my schooldays: it was the face of Dr. Racketts, my old headmaster, a face which shone now in the sunlight as it always had shone, the mild eyes beaming through round, polished spectacles. He had a tall, well-made figure, whose dignity always seemed to be belied by the round, slightly feminine features, the gentle moustache, and the lifeless way in which a few frail strands of sandy hair hung down towards his right eyebrow.

Dr. Racketts had taken us in the sixth form for a subject of his own devising known as "Philosophical Background," which was supposed to win growing minds over to sympathy with the Christian point of view, whilst avoiding any kind of dogmatic indoctrination and shunning any reference to the miraculous. He had so long and so consistently evaded all that was controversial in Christian teaching that he had eventually ceased to commit himself to anything at all—except to the reiteration of platitudinous ethical principles so generally acceptable as to require no defence. His evasion of what he called "denominational sectarianism" was designed to make his course pleasing to pupils of all varieties of religious or irreligious backgrounds. In fact, of course, it had the opposite effect. Committed Christians were continually irritated by the diluted misrepresentation of the Christian position, whilst atheists and agnostics were rendered increasingly hostile to a faith which turned out to be nothing more than a collection of milk-and-water platitudes.

Poor Dr. Racketts had gradually become so obsessed with the perils of controversy and disagreement that his whole life of teaching and administration had ultimately become dominated by the habit of pretending that differences and difficulties did not exist. In the name of tolerance he blurred all doctrinal issues, and in the name of charity he submerged conflicting policies in a bog of inactivity. He had learned to smooth over every problem, intellectual or administrative, by sentimental utterances about the family spirit, decorated by indulgent sighs. And here now was Squash—of course he was known to everyone as Squash—hand in hand with the wife of an archdeacon, and beaming genially up at me from a valley bottom in Paradise.

I waved weakly in response to a signal, feeling anew that sense of boredom with which I had once approached his lessons. Then, suddenly conscious of displaying no enthusiasm, I tried to make amends and got up from my seat.

"Shall we go to meet them?"

"It is the proper thing to do," said Lamiel. "They will not have any difficulty in getting across to this side. It ought to be a merry meeting."

There was reason to say this for, as we wound our way down the bank, knee deep in bracken, giggles and laughter marked the unsteady progress of the couple from stone to stone across the stream. There are some people who are never happy without an audience, and who assume an audience even when it is lacking. Squash could turn anything into a public performance. Indeed, he couldn't stick a stamp on an envelope without a bang and a little speech. He lived self-consciously in the public eye, even when the public was absent, bored or asleep. A last exultant cry and a peal of masculine laughter advertised the arrival of the two upon our side of the stream, and as we came upon them, they still stood hand in hand, laughing towards each other a laugh of mutual self-display which was positively embarrassing for the onlookers, at whom it was unmistakably directed.

"Let me introduce Mrs. Templecombe," said Squash.

"We have met," I said. "We were examined together a short time ago. This is my Guardian, Lamiel."

Lamiel bowed slightly with his accustomed dignity, but Squash burst out into forced, nervous laughter again. Then he suddenly caught the look of grave imperturbability on Lamiel's face, and in a flash the wide circular grin vanished from his mouth and a simpering tightening of the lips replaced it. Accompanied by an affected lowering of the eyelids, this change in the features seemed to indicate officially that a mood of formal piety ought now to replace the boisterous gaiety of a moment ago. My embarrassment increased. I half expected Squash to sigh out "Let us pray!" as he used to do in the school chapel long ago; but instead he breathed in a soothing tone, "I have found a friend. You will know what that means to me."

I'm afraid I could but dimly conjecture what it meant to him. Having already formed an impression of Mrs. Templecombe, I suspected that it might easily spell utter disaster for him. However, I had long ago learned to assume an expression of passive interest when being spoken to by Squash; so I merely nodded, hoping in vain that he wouldn't enlarge upon the subject.

"We see eye to eye," he said, "and how comforting that is. I have met so many up here who lack sympathy and understanding. These angels—they are nice people in a way—but so narrow, so doctrinaire. They will dogmatize. They try to bring you round to their particular point of view; and people with narrow attachments to fixed ideas cause such unpleasantness in the long run. They break up the family spirit; and it's so important to keep the right atmosphere, especially up here where there are so many people trying to indoctrinate others with their ideas. I have learned to distrust ideas. I think personal relationships so much more important, don't you?"

Lamiel, to whom this question was addressed, answered in patient, measured tones.

"The value of personal relationships depends upon whether they are good relationships or bad ones. And I am afraid that the concepts 'good' and 'bad' belong to that realm of ideas which you find so dangerous."

"Oh, but of course," said Mrs. Templecombe, "he means good relationships. How could he mean otherwise?"

"We mustn't argue about these things," said Squash earnestly. "I never did believe in arguments. They only lead to divisions of opinion, which destroy the family spirit. I always smoothed over all arguments in my school. That was what made it such a happy one. We set our faces against bigotry and dogmatism and all disagreements. We forgot all controversies of opinion in a life of common endeavour. We all kept our private ideas to ourselves. That is real tolerance."

"It requires no great exercise of tolerance," said Lamiel, "to put up with hostile opinions that are not uttered."

"We lived in the spirit of true fellowship," said Squash, ignoring Lamiel's irony. "Our life together was rich in personal harmony. Those with fixed ideas learned to forget them in working as a band of brothers. Perhaps we missed something in academic achievement; but there never was a happier and more

Christian school. Could a man do more than that?"

"I should like to know," said Lamiel quietly, "whether your employers paid you a salary on the understanding that you would do your best to educate your pupils in the culture of the mind. That knowledge would put me in a better position to judge your case."

Now Squash always had a genius for that convenient kind of irrelevance which is so shattering as to leave one's opponent speechless. So it was that he burst out lyrically in an attack upon covetousness, which no one had defended.

"What does a salary matter? It is sad to see so many people worrying their heads about what they can earn—especially people in a profession called to labour for others. Money does not bring happiness. It is personal relationships that bring joy to a man."

"I only wish," said Mrs. Templecombe, "that you could have known my husband, the archdeacon. What great work you might have done together. But you shall see him soon. The meeting will be a privilege for both of you. How fine—and how rare—to see two Christians meeting together."

"My own experience," said Lamiel, "for what it is worth, is that it is difficult to get away from Christians in this particular environment."

"He was a great humanizer," went on Mrs. Templecombe, unheeding. "Human beings come first, he always used to say. That's so true, isn't it?"

"There is a school of thought up here," said Lamiel, "which finds it difficult to reconcile that view with the view that God should come first."

"Human beings," said Squash, warming to the subject, "personal relationships, the life of common endeavour, the family spirit. It all amounts to the same thing. It's just—well, it's just Christianity."

"The correct term," said Lamiel, "is *humanism*, I believe."

"That's right," said Mrs. Templecombe. "*Humanist* is the word. Christ was the first great humanist. That is what my husband used to say."

"If only," said Squash with a sigh, "if only we could re-create here the spirit of fellowship which permeated my school. It is so badly needed. We are all brothers, after all, and must learn to live together as such. Yet there is dreadful intolerance here. Hundreds of thousands of people live as outcasts in the cities of the damned, as they are called. The Hierarchies have cut us off from them. They have erected an iron curtain which makes communication very difficult. But we have a very fine association here which is re-establishing contact with these poor souls. I am devoting all my efforts to the service of this association, which is doing all it can to improve relationships with the outcasts. We don't want to influence them in their opinions, of course; that wouldn't be fair. They have a perfect right to hold what views they please. It is true that their ideas are out of favour with the Hierarchies, and their attitudes too. But that is no reason for cutting them off. Our association is determined to show them that we are united by common interests and sympathies which transcend these petty differences, and make them negligible. We have a thriving new branch of the association in Helicon. If you are going there, you must join at once."

"I am not exactly free to do just what I want there," I said, with a side glance at Lamiel.

"Well, you must join in the great work if the opportunity should come later on. There is a notice on the door—*Society for Cultural Relations with the Damned*. They have made me a travelling secretary. That is why I am in a position to show Mrs. Templecombe her way about."

"He has promised very kindly to help me find my husband," said Mrs. Templecombe.

"I think we had better continue on our way," said Lamiel, abruptly terminating the conversation. "You, I gather, are going to Fordshaw."

"Yes," said Mrs. Templecombe. "Are we not going in the right direction?"

"Up the bank and over the ridge," said Lamiel, pointing out the way. "When you run up against the cart track, turn right and you will soon join the main road to Fordshaw. We are going there ourselves later, when my ward has seen Helicon."

Good-byes were said, and as the two left us to climb the hill, we scrambled across the stream and made our way in the opposite direction. We climbed the bank in silence, and it was not until we were treading a wide, rough track over the brow of the hill that I ventured to speak. I began to apologize for Squash.

"He's a very decent sort," I said, "but he just hasn't got the right ideas."

"Whilst you, who *have* got the right ideas..."

"Oh, I know, I know. But all that stuff about personal relationships."

"Not utterly hollow," said Lamiel. "You may have observed that he was truly glad to see you, whilst you..."

"I was always bored by him. That's quite true."

"And quite deplorable. Moreover, I doubt whether *he* is now engaged in passing judgment upon *you*."

"I know. I've said that kind of thing to myself many a time."

"You've said far too much to yourself. I might remark that you have swamped yourself with useful information and gratuitous good advice. The self, the true self—the will, if you like, has been immobilized by the burden."

I was silent for a few moments, feeling a good deal humbled, but eventually I ventured another reference to Squash.

"Isn't he engaged on rather dangerous work?" I asked.

"It is not good for him; but less dangerous than it would be for most people. He is protected by an intrinsic good-heartedness; and that is a protection not granted to everyone."

The rebuke went home, and I tried to make amends.

"Therefore I ought not to judge him, I suppose."

"Therefore this conversation is quite fruitless," said Lamiel. "Comparative evaluations of your own spiritual state and the spiritual state of others can only injure you. Shallow ground, stony ground, thorny ground: it is all one for rendering the seed fruitless."

4

Helicon impressed me from the first as a quiet city. We entered it by a gateway, medieval in appearance, and found ourselves in a narrow lane between high walls, which allowed no view of anything save the sky overhead. My curiosity was aroused at once by the blankness of these walls, but the lane wound round to the right ahead of us, so that nothing at all could be seen of the city's magnificence, which they concealed. I say "magnificence" because this was the quality which I sensed and, along with the tranquillity of the place, it filled me with a kind of awe. However, as we rounded the next bend in the lane, and still saw nothing but blank walls, I began to wonder whether there *was* in fact any real magnificence about the place to justify my feeling of awe. As I examined myself about the basis of this feeling, it occurred to me that I was perhaps the victim of a subjective delusion. I had lived in an ancient city for many years: I naturally associated high walls of this kind with magnificent old residences surrounded by rich, secluded gardens. Suppose I had lived most of my life in some drab industrial area, under the shadow of a vast gaol, and had never known familiarly the great walls of an ancient city, should I in that case have sensed magnificence now?

"I think you would," said Lamiel quietly.

I started, as I always did when he suddenly showed that he had clearly read my thoughts.

"The question is a philosophical one," he went on. "You sense magnificence around you. Is it a given magnificence, dwelling inherently in the objects of your environment, or have you created it from the imaginative scrap of your own past experience—and then imposed it upon the present environment? You incline to the view that qualities like magnificence do in fact inhere in the objective order. You were always more of a realist than an idealist, I think. I hope these are the right terms. Your modern philosophical terminology confuses me a little."

"In that sense, I am a realist," I said, "though I don't claim to understand fully the various doctrines of value. But I have a sceptical strain."

"All realists are sceptical; especially Christian realists. They cannot get away with the idea that man has created his own values by spewing over the universe the undigested nourishment of his own animal appetites. They are sceptical about man's supposed capacity to vomit so productively. You know just enough philosophy to appreciate the point, I think. Yet you were on the verge of attributing your present awe to an odd accident of youth. You have been reading the educational psychologists."

"I'm grateful to have my philosophical error pointed out. I'm glad the fault is of an academic kind this time."

"Oh, dear, no," said Lamiel. "How readily you

jump to unwarranted conclusions. Your mistake now is an even graver one. I said the question was a philosophical one, but I never said that your act of distrust had the nature of a philosophical error. That is not the case at all. Your logic is much weaker than I thought. Intellectual discussion of the nature of value is, of course, a philosophical matter. But you were not engaged in such a discussion—not even with yourself. You were engaged in distrusting a given value. There was an act of the will, directed towards the obliteration of that value. The question may be a philosophical one, but your act was a moral act—or rather an immoral act."

"Can this distinction be pressed home?"

"It certainly can. Many a philosopher, who has on paper explained away all human values in terms of subjective desire and subjective delusion, has actually lived in fanatical devotion to values residing in the objective order—the value of truth, for instance. That being so, you may imagine that it would not be difficult to find examples of the converse."

My reply was forestalled by the sound of distant music. For a second I halted; but the sound faded and we walked on again, still enclosed by high walls, though we had made one or two turns, to left and to right, whilst talking together.

"You paused, for some reason," said Lamiel a few moments later.

"I thought I heard music."

"Perhaps you did hear it."

It came again, clearer and louder; strings, brass—yes, and voices too. At that moment we rounded a last bend in the lane and the sound was explained. There, rising before us, stood a great church, a cathedral in dimension and in dignity. We were facing what appeared to be the west doors. Two twin towers rose before us, and the square block of a mighty central tower, even higher than they, could be seen between them. On our left a path ran diagonally across a wide lawn and disappeared in a bunch of trees. Beyond the trees, towers, roofs and chimneys marked what appeared to be the centre of the city of Helicon. We stopped and listened. The music was vaguely familiar and I have always liked to test myself at identification, though I realized that this time there would be no announcer to confirm my guess at the end.

"Beethoven," I said, and a moment afterwards I knew that I was right. "The Mass in D."

"Yes, they are fond of public concerts. There is a great deal of culture in Helicon; perhaps too much, but I leave you to judge that for yourself."

"And the cathedral—are the services here like those on earth?"

"Exactly—if by 'here' you mean in Helicon. Elsewhere, in more blessed cities, there are differences."

My curiosity was roused, and I rushed headlong into the next question.

"In these more blessed cities is there anything equivalent to the Mass?"

"There is something corresponding to it; but, as I have just said, there are differences."

"What are they?"

"The sort of differences you might expect. You were brought up to a tradition of the Eucharist which involved the doctrine of the Real Presence. There are conditions under which the Presence might be, not only Real, but manifestly Real. That is enough."

Lamiel spoke quietly and without drama; and I reflected in silence for a few moments on what this
might mean. I thought of Our Lord as Himself the
sacrificing High Priest. Did Lamiel mean that the cel-
ebrant became visibly *that* in the acts of oblation and
consecration? Or could he possibly refer to something
much more terrible and frightening—some unthinkable visible connection between the Broken Body and
the Food of Communion?

"I don't fully understand what you mean," I said. "I
just can't picture it."

"Of course you can't. It is almost a blasphemy to
try. If you are going to spend your time trying to picture such things, then there must be no talk of them at
all. Patient and submissive waiting upon a yet-to-be-
experienced mystery is one thing: curious and undisci-
plined imaging of the future revelation is a very
different thing, and a distinctly unhealthy thing too.
These things are as far apart as mysticism and spiritu-
alism."

As Lamiel spoke, we had begun to walk across the
lawns on our left towards the knoll of trees which hid
the city. Occasionally I turned, as we walked, to admire the solid length of the great church, the more
solid in appearance for the geometrical neatness with
which it sat squarely against the flat, trimmed lawns.

"The place brings back memories?" said Lamiel in
a questioning tone.

"Nothing clear or particular," I replied. "It is just
generally reminiscent of a small English Cathedral
city."

"That's because it *is* a Cathedral city—or the nearest approach we have here to that kind of thing. You

are being taken to visit the College for Gnostics. Where else would you expect to find gnostics, if not in something like a Cathedral city?"

He smiled in that rather sad fashion of his, which always seemed to imply that, while the joke ought to be enjoyed, its grave pointedness ought not to be over-looked.

"Properly speaking," he went on, "it is not a cathedral, for there is no bishopric here and nothing corresponding to one. But the minister has about a hundred residentiary canonries, largely held by clergy who have been placed in the College for Gnostics. The number of canonries may surprise you. Formerly there were only fifty, but we had to double the number recently in order to provide for the rising intake of gnostic clergy. However, we reckon that the peak has been reached. You know yourself that there are signs of the change for the better in this matter down below. We hope to be able to reduce the number of canonries shortly. Most freshmen in orders now belong to the age-groups born between 1880 and 1900—men who were studying at the universities in that very bad patch between 1900 and 1920. These age-groups have produced what we call the Gnostic Bulge, which puts great pressure upon us here. In the Backward Believers' Department at Fordshaw they complain of a Modernist Bulge which covers roughly the same age-groups. I am no statistician and must rely largely on hearsay in this matter, but I understand that bulges in quite different heresies are shortly expected."

"Am I to understand that the College for Gnostics is largely filled with clergy?"

"Ordained priests and professional ministers of the Gospel are in a majority here. But other intellectual professions are well represented too."

We were through the trees now and were walking in a street. There were a few passers-by, but the general impression remained one of quiet. I think this impression was largely due to the complete absence of any wheeled traffic, and also, as I realized later, to the notable lack of shops.

As we first came among the buildings of Helicon, I was immensely impressed by the beauty of the place—and more so by that quality of charm which arouses sensations of nostalgia. There were no modern buildings, and none in the nineteenth-century style. Every house appeared to belong either to the eighteenth century or to an earlier period—and most of them to the Tudor or Elizabethan Ages. There was no special architectural congruity between the buildings which lined the street—but there was a congruity in atmosphere, for they all smacked of romantic antiquity. White walls interlaced by sturdy black timbers, odd gables, multiform ornamented chimney stacks, bow-windows of every conceivable antique style, square Georgian fronts, brass knockers, lamps of decorated wrought iron—everything combined to give the impression of historical richness. Yet all was well preserved; roofs in good repair, woodwork freshly painted, brass-work well polished, and everything spick-and-span. It was as though the whole place was being cared for by a Superlunary Office of Works as a Complete Set of Historical Monuments.

"It is all extremely old," I said.

"It appears to be," Lamiel replied. "But in fact a good deal of it is of fairly recent construction. The city authorities will allow only buildings which 'harmonize.' That means only buildings which smack of the eighteenth century or earlier. Craftsmen cultivate the ancient styles in building and equipping these places—even, I may say, at the cost of convenience, hygiene and often of sound construction. No one would pretend that these preposterous windows and chimneys are functional—or even beautiful, considered in isolation: but they all contribute to the general impression. There is a great centre here for the Preservation of Ancient Crafts. Had your educational interests been different, I might have been able to show you."

We turned to the right, down what appeared, by its width, to be the main street of the city. I was struck, as we walked, by the repeated appearance of neat little notices on the walls of the buildings. Some were polished brass plates and some carven marble, but most were black wooden boards with white lettering upon them in the Gothic style. Lamiel was quite content to sauter on more slowly as I showed signs of interesting myself in the city, and I took the opportunity of reading one of these notices.

> Here smote Hecqhild the serf
> his own liegelord Sir Trevis.
> The damosel Etrenne she saw
> it and wept
> for there was mickle blood.

This, I believe, was the first thing to shake my admiration for Helicon. It suggested a habit of cultivating the antique, which was too artificial and self-conscious to be healthy. I felt that there must be a deficiency in the sense of humour of the people who preserved the museumlike quality of the place. This was a feeling which recurred many times before I ended my visit.

And a glance at other notices nearby confirmed my new suspicions. One ran thus—

> Sir Morbille de Morbille
> took his ease at this hostelrie
> on the Eve of the Joyous Jousting
> at Belle Avis
> whereat he did matchless feats
> of arms.

and another—

> This ground gave King Richard
> to his trusty tailor Wat Snipkin
> together with once a year at
> Martinmass a haunch of venison
> from his royal park at Whitkirk
> and two hogskins of good red wine.

As I looked further afield, I realized that, in some form or other, every building had its little notice. In some cases it appeared that brains had been severely racked to find a significant event to commemorate—and not always with much success, for I read one notice which ran,

> John William Smith dwelt here
> in the fear of the Lord,
> who now dwelleth elsewhere.

I found the grammar of this slightly ambiguous and the message unilluminating; and there were even modester claims on other notices. I may mention—

> Judith Bottomley lives here
> and she keeps a good house.

But the least controversial of all the notices had a peculiar provocative directness—

𝔥𝔢𝔯𝔢 (𝔇. 𝔙.) 𝔡𝔴𝔢𝔩𝔩 𝔍
𝔊𝔞𝔦𝔫𝔰𝔞𝔶 𝔦𝔱 𝔴𝔥𝔬 𝔴𝔦𝔩𝔩.

Not being anxious to involve myself in fruitless altercation, I turned from this, and Lamiel directed my attention to a more informative legend nearby, which I should have been sorry to miss, though its message was moral rather than historical.

HELICON HISTORICAL SOCIETY

Below is a faithful transcript of verses inscribed upon an ancient piece of parchment which was discovered in the chimney-piece of this house. The verses are believed to represent the sole remaining fragment of the famous Gondalic epic cycle, Hrotgar's Revenge. The text was deciphered by Professor Montegall.

> Whan Mistris Nan her son ybore
> Sche brast him straight upon the floor
> And then, poor bairn, he was namoore.
> Now learn by this, if ye have wytt,
> Nor nurse your burthen nor foster ytt—
> Ere it wax great, see ye be quytt!

"But this is antiquarianism run riot," I said in astonishment.

"It is one of the more extreme examples of Heliconian eccentricity," said Lamiel, "and for that reason I wished you to see it. But we need not delay longer. You have sampled now a feature of the city which may assist you in forming a general impression."

Lamiel led me down the main street, which eventually broadened out into a spacious square. As we walked, I was struck by the lack of shops, but there were several cafés, exaggeratedly antique in appearance. One was distinguished by a monstrous piece of painted kitchenware suspended over the doorway, and a notice—*Ye signe of ye Copper Kettle*. Lamiel drew my attention to it.

"It is an ingenious contrivance. When it rains, the drains from the roof carry a certain amount of water into the huge kettle. The thing is skillfully balanced so that the water soon begins to pour from the spout upon passers-by. Along with the minster, this is probably the most visited feature of interest in Helicon. There is invariably a small crowd at this point on a wet day."

We passed by, and my attention was attracted by what appeared to be a single stall in this wide marketplace. As we drew near, I saw that it was nothing but a great table laden with paperbacked books. A notice invited visitors to take one, and I accepted the invitation. The book was a gaudily-produced brochure, entitled *Guide to Helicon*. It was illustrated with numerous photographs and pencil sketches. I caught sight of the minster and the copper kettle as I flicked over the pages.

"You will find that a very adequate introduction to the city," said Lamiel, "but you will not have time to inspect the many treasures advertised there."

I continued to turn the pages as we walked.

The ancient city of Helicon, once metropolis of Westernia, keeps still its old dignity and charm. Situated in a rich valley, between stretches of rolling downland, it may justly claim to be the loveliest retreat in Paradise. Its well-preserved buildings are gems torn from the diadem of history. Its streets, thus pricelessly decked out, effuse an atmosphere redolent of age-old wonder.

Among the most famous features of interest are the magnificent minster, whose every stone tells a story of past grandeur, and the ancient College for Gnostics, ever true to the inspiring motto of its founder— MOLEHILLS MAKYTH MOUNTAINS.

The College is renowned for its warm-hearted hospitality, and a cordial welcome awaits interested well-wishers from near or far. Intending visitors should queue up three-deep at the Tradesmen's Entrance in Fishgate Passage. When a party of thirty has gathered, they will be shown around the outside walls by the under-porter's assistant.

Admission Fee: Adults 5/, Children 3/6.

Proceeds for the Dons' Buttery Fund.

Turning the pages further, I learned something of the contents of the city's thirty-five museums. I gathered that four of these housed treasures of antiquity discovered in the vicinity; and that the other thirty-one were devoted to relics of past scholars who had adorned the life of Helicon College. In a section devoted to the social amenities of the city, a prominent place was given to the activities of the Helicon Madrigal Club, the Helicon Place-Names Society, the Helicon Archaeological Association, the Helicon Arts Society, the Socratic Circle and the Eighteenth-century Club.

A little further on I found some interesting notes about the surrounding countryside.

WALKS AROUND HELICON

The countryside around Helicon is rich in interest both for the naturalist and for the antiquarian. On hills within convenient walking-distance of the city centre are to be found numerous ancient barrows, tumuli, earthworks, burial grounds and encampments. These have been specially constructed by the Helicon Archaeological Association, at great expense. No effort has been spared to ensure that they should be faithful historical monuments, exact in every detail. This magnificent piece of historical reconstruction, carried out with the active support of the City Fathers, has brought within the compass of Heliconian residents memorials of the past which cannot fail to speak to the soul of man.

As I hastily ran my fingers through the remaining pages of the book, a loose paper fell floating to the ground. I picked it up, and found it to be a leaflet specially inserted to catch the visitor's eye; and I read it with some interest.

HELICON SPECIAL APPEAL FUND FOR THE PRESERVATION AND RENOVATION OF ANCIENT CHURCHES

Helicon is rich in ancient parish churches of unique architectural and historical interest. A number of these churches are now unfortunately in a bad state of repair.

Funds are urgently needed to restore them to their former glory. In many cases the fabric requires extensive rebuilding. Some of the buildings need to be re-roofed. In the interest of public safety, repairs cannot long be delayed. If you care for these treasures of our civilization, you can show your concern by contributing to our fund.

THIS APPEAL IS DIRECTED TO ALL UNRESERVEDLY

It must be emphasized that these churches no longer serve the limited needs of any one sect or creed. In agreeing to combine together to make this appeal, we have stipulated that the buildings in question shall in future be used only for services which have no religious significance whatsoever. The authorities concerned have magnanimously accepted this condition. We are therefore able to unite in a call to all men of goodwill who value our common inheritance.

F. Z. THURSTHISTLE, Principal of Helicon College.

E. G. BACKWATER, President of Helicon Ethical Union.

U. P. WISDOM, Secretary of Helicon Rationalist Circle.

A. J. RATT, Rector of Thorp-cum-Addleby and Wallash with Pendlehutt.

As I read this, the two of us came to a standstill. A short avenue, leading off to the right from the bottom of the square, had brought us face to face with a building which looked for all the world like a college in one of our ancient university cities. Lamiel paused at the foot of a wide flight of steps which led up to the main entrance.

"Do you wish to ask me any questions before we go in?"

"One thing I'd like to know," I said. "The pupils here are obviously not students preparing for examinations on the brink of their careers, and I gather that they are not exactly under instruction. I suppose the place is a kind of graduate institution, like All Souls."

"That is rather hard on All Souls; but you are on the right lines. The members here are responsible as a body for arranging their own studies. They pursue research individually and they come together for lectures given by the more distinguished members of the college. The opportunity to read papers and lead discussions is offered to all at some time or another. The

largest audiences are drawn by members who are distinguished—either by the importance of the position
they reached in earthly life, or by the length of their
service in the college. There is no direct instruction
given by the Hierarchies. Indeed, if pupils were ready
for such instruction, they would no longer be in place
in this establishment. When a member shows a real
desire for such instruction, he is removed elsewhere.
At that stage the course is considered to have done its
work. Meantime, members engage in intellectual pursuits within the college as they would at a university
below. In their leisure time the more earnest occupy
themselves in the various cultural activities for which
Helicon is renowned. For the less serious there is an
endless round of Sherry parties and Bridge parties—
though this particular kind of activity is not publicly
advertised. It is something one becomes aware of
through living in the place."

"And the residentiary canons?"

"They of course, fulfil regular duties in the minster.
The work is not onerous."

"There is something depressing about the picture
you have given me," I said, musing aloud. "It seems to
confirm the crude view of eternal life as a mere exten-
sion of earthly existence—existence with nothing more
than an earthly quality, I mean."

"I'm afraid that is a fairly just description of life in
Helicon."

"It sounds so hopeless. Isn't there anything to remind Heliconians of the *possibilities* of life elsewhere—in the more blessed cities you told me of?"

"There is no one here who was not visited through-
out his earthly life by the usual series of visions, some
fitful, some more abiding, but all pointing clearly to

those possibilities of which you speak. The pecularity of gnostics, as you will discover, is that they explain away all visions by a process of intellectual dissection. Insofar as they receive illuminations, they interpret them at the cerebral level, and the will is untouched. That is precisely what it means to be a gnostic."

"They had their Guardians to put them right."

"They *had* their Guardians. But they would not grant their Guardians the compliment of taking their existence seriously. Now, therefore, they are the most part left to themselves. Or it would be more proper to say that they have cut themselves off. At any rate, their Guardians have been withdrawn. A return to wardship is what we offer them. Once they are prepared to accept our guardianship again, their course here is over. But of course you can't accept the guardianship of someone whose existence is in doubt."

We mounted the flight of steps and entered the Porter's Lodge. Lamiel stopped for a few moments to study various notices pinned on the boards, and I stared into a great cloistered quadrangle whose neat lawn was bisected by a flagged path directly in front of me. At the far end of the path a clock tower rose above a pillared portico, which broke the otherwise unbroken series or arches around the quadrangle.

"We can see the college at work," said Lamiel, turning from the board; and he led me across the quadrangle, under the portico and into a long stone corridor which was flanked on the right-hand side by a series of square-looking doorways. Choosing one of these, he listened intently for some time with his hand on the knob, and then quietly led me inside. Quietly I slid into an empty seat at the back of what appeared to be a public meeting, and Lamiel stood behind my chair.

There were about fifty people sitting in front of me, and, on a platform before us, half-a-dozen men faced this audience in a semicircle. In the middle, a slim be-spectacled man—apparently the chairman—presided at a table, equipped with the usual glass of water and supply of writing-paper. The person on his left was standing and addressing the meeting. He was a short, rather stout individual with a bald head and a placid gaze. His big eyes dispensed tranquillity; his thin mouth cut a rather incongruous straight furrow across a smooth and pouchy face.

"It is fitting," he was saying, in a smooth, mellifluous voice, rather high-pitched but eminently gentlemanly, "it is fitting that a speaker who addresses others on a subject like this should make his personal history known. For twenty years I was headmaster of a distinguished and ancient Public School, responsible for the education of some of the noblest and most cultivated young minds in the land. For the last ten years of my headmastership I was an ordained minister, committed by my profession to the essential truth of Christianity. In me, therefore, two distinct traditions met; for, as a headmaster, I stood as the representative of liberal humanism and, as a minister, I stood as the representative of the Gospel of Christ.

"Let me first explain what it means to be an honest educator. Bred in my bone was that devotion to free enquiry which is the marrow of Western Culture. I stood for the unfettered freedom of the aspiring human intellect. I stood also for that principle of intellectual tolerance which forbids any scholar to enter into argument holding the presupposition that his opponent is in the wrong. I stood for the unassailable truth—the very foundation of all science and scholar-

ship—that many windows in the temple of man's
thought bring light from the eternal source of all Wisdom: and I clung with resolution to the conviction
that we must fearlessly accept whatever illumination
is granted to man's reason, whether through the clear,
plain windows of scientific discovery, the ornamented
windows of imaginative art, or the dim, coloured
windows of philosophical speculation and religious
revelation. I would not allow that any window should
be curtained, even though its light seemed to render
dim and unreal the illuminations granted through the
stained-glass panes of religious tradition. I was ready
always to meet new truth, however harsh and unpal-
atable. No unalterable dogma could lurk in the chaste
chambers of my God-given reason.

"Yet I was—I am—a Christian minister, avowing
the truth of Christianity. How, you may ask, did I reconcile these conflicting roles?

"The answer is that I did not reconcile them; for the
two positions are in fact irreconcilable. The honest
teacher must be prepared, if he takes the name of
Christian, to exist in a state of tension, bearing the
burden of man's ignorance; for this is the Cross laid
upon the shoulders of the fearless scholar. The Truth is
not yet known to us: we must be prepared to accept
glimpses of it wherever man's increasing knowledge
searches it out. New truth may repel us, but we must
not falter. That was my fundamental position as a
humble scholar in the tradition of a great humane culture. But there was a qualification, a subordinate
principle—an amendment, if you like—attached to
this central pillar of my thought. It was this. For the
present, in our state of ignorance, we must accept the
most rational hypothesis which can give, if not a se-

cure account of the meaning of life, at least a firm basis for personal conduct. And this is what I found in Christianity. This led me to the Church. Here was a philosophy which offered a working hypothesis, a temporary anchorage, an interim security. Here was something to nourish my soul and guide my footsteps until the real truth could be known. Here was a sublime imaginative interpretation of the meaning of the universe and the role of man therein. Here was a foundation for morality, an inspiration to endeavour and a consolation in distress. Here was a crown of mystic sanction upon the noble philosophy of Plato, a synthesis which drew together his transcendent values in the figure of one Absolute Wisdom, eternal and divine.

"Greatest, most daring dream of all, here was a comprehensive theory of existence which might turn out to be nearer to the truth than any other scheme of man's imagining.

"My position is substantially the same today. I see no reason for making any radical change in the position which I adopted ten years ago when I requested the Bishop to admit me to Holy Orders. Now, as then, I believe Christianity to offer the best working hypothesis, the soundest basis for altruistic moral conduct.

"The question under discussion this morning has already been plainly stated by the Chairman—'How has the recent experience of hon. members modified their views of the Christian Faith?' I have given the core of my answer directly. Radically my faith remains unshaken, with all its daring unsubstantiated claims. But I should be less than honest if I allowed my statement to end there. No man who faces the truth can undergo striking new experiences without adapting his convictions to the illuminations which they bring. I must confess, therefore, that in some less fundamental respects, I am today a sadder and a wiser man.

"First, I must admit to a feeling of disappointment. Hanging on as I did, through years of intellectual stress, to the Christian hypothesis, I hoped for some reward this side the grave. I do not mean that I ever anticipated an indulgence in those celestial comestibles vulgarly referred to as 'pie in the sky.' But I expected to find my faith here corroborated and confirmed. I believe that I express the feelings of many in the present audience, when I say that the lack of corroboration here of Christian teaching is a grievous disappointment." (Several voices here interposed a quiet "Here, hear!") "Nevertheless, I am not one of those who believe that we ought to pass a formal vote of censure upon the celestial authorities for leaving us thus in uncertainty—for we have all learned much in the hard school of uncertainty. Indeed, we have always distrusted certainty. The uncertainty of the Christian hypothesis was the fire in which our intellects and our moral wills were tested and proven." (This remark provoked a louder series of "Hear, hears!" and one or two brief outbursts of clapping.) "We have, of course, the right and the duty to put on record our disappointment with the provisions made for us in this respect. But there is no cause for us to abandon that position of faith in uncertainty, which sustained us in our labours below. For, if there is here no overt corroboration of the Christian hypothesis, there is certainly no direct refutation of it. We refuse, therefore, to evade in cowardice the tremendous tension of clinging still to the Christian hypothesis, against a background of sustained intellectual doubt."

An outburst of enthusiastic applause at this point showed that the audience were generally in sympathy with the speaker's declaration. Several of the listeners lifted their heads and straightened their backs, as if in response to a challenge to their personal courage and steadfastness. The speaker was visibly heartened as he continued.

"I have only one more point to make. Your generous support emboldens me to make it clearly and fearlessly. It is this. I fought all my life against those obscurantists and superstitious bigots who regarded the Christian Church as an institution with a specific divine authority. I regarded the Church always as a society of earnest seekers after truth. On this comparatively trivial question, my experience on this side of the grave has confirmed my attitude and put its propriety beyond doubt. There is no mystic authority in priesthood and sacrament, no distinctly supernatural character in the ordinances of a Christian institution. Here we find the Church exactly as it was on earth—a brotherhood of men who have agreed to accept a common hypothesis. We now find ourselves cut off from our brothers on the earth, as they are cut off from us. There is no hint of a Supernatural Body uniting us across the barriers of the grave. We, as they, are called to go fearlessly forward, carrying on in a new sphere that quest for truth which is man's privilege and his burden. The spirit of man is unconquerable. Believing where we cannot prove, and proving where we have ceased to believe, we shall tread the paths of eternity with the dauntless confidence which sustained us below. We were there a light to those we taught, and we are not therefore unpractised in opening the eyes of the blind. There is no less need here for that message of hope which the witness of the illumined mind can bring to the bewildered and the disconsolate."

As the speaker sat down, the audience burst again into fervent applause. Several listeners repeated "Hear, hear!" several times and a few enthusiasts cheered vociferously. When the noise subsided, the chairman rose to address the meeting. He spoke in suave and cultivated tones, measuring his words, not with tenative nervousness, but with the deliberation of a man who is thoroughly at ease.

"There is small cause for me to express the gratitude of this meeting to Canon Hugh Mandrake. You have shown your approval unmistakably. I had the privilege for many years of working as one of Mandrake's colleagues at Carchester. I had therefore good reason for selecting him today as the speaker best fitted to make the final speech from the platform. I relied upon him to rally us at the last with a call to courageous perseverance; and I was not disappointed. I relied upon him too to sum up the general feelings of the meeting—platform and audience alike—and again I was not disappointed. He has made it unnecessary for me to spend time in summing up the general trend of the discussion. One or two points only need to be highlighted. First, we have detected in the speeches a general sense of disappointment at the absence of corroboration of the Christian Faith in our present environment. But underlying that sense of disappointment is a firm determination to cling to the Christian hypothesis. Thus the answer given by the platform to the question under discussion is clear and forthright. Recent experience of hon. members has not radically affected their intellectual position. But each speaker has hinted at modifications of his attitude in subsidiary

matters. The general trend of these modifications is
clearly discernible. It is towards increased distrust of
the supernatural claims made by the Christian
Church as an institution. The line which we adopted
on earth has been justified and confirmed in this respect. We have every cause to pin our faith even more
strongly to the enquiring human intellect, and to distrust everything in revelation and in ecclesiastical tradition which would seduce us from open enquiry or
fetter us with the false claims of a mystical sanction.

"And now some of you gentlemen who have listened
so patiently may like to ask questions or to make com-
ments. Please do so."

The chairman sat down and a low buzz of conversation developed on the floor of the house. Very soon a
venerable bearded gentleman rose to his feet.

"Professor Dendrane," said the chairman.

"Gentlemen," said the professor in a quavering and
rather querulous voice, "as the latest arrival here I can
claim to speak with up-to-the minute authority. One
argument which is being increasingly used by informed Christian apologists below seems to me to have
been unjustifiably neglected. It is pre-eminently the
argument of the nineteen-fifties, and as such ought to
have a sympathetic hearing, for even here we must
strive to keep up to date.... The optimism of humanis-
tic liberalism, so congenial to the nineteenth century,
with all its commercial prosperity, was proved
groundless by the diabolical wars and political revolu-
tions of the twentieth century. The doctrine of inevitable scientific progress, also congenial to the inventive
nineteenth century, became a hollow theory in the age
of atomic warfare. The promising psychological studies of the nineteenth century proved, in my own time,

to be incapable of adding fundamentally to our understanding of the human spirit. Nineteenth-century aesthetic hedonism petered out in clinical neurosis and in morbid artistic decadence. And lastly, nineteenth-century materialism committed cultural suicide in the form of twentieth-century communism. What remained but the Christian Faith? What other view of life could cater for an age of wars and upheavals; what other philosophy could meet the needs of an age of malaise and disillusionment? It was on these grounds that I, as a professor of Theology, recommended Christianity to the young. On the same grounds I bid you, here in this bewildering habitation, to hold fast to your faith. Gentlemen, no rational alternative is offered us; for none is known, even below."

A low murmur of approval came from some quarters as the professor sat down. I turned and whispered to Lamiel behind me.

"Don't any of these people simply believe in Christian Faith just because it's true?"

Lamiel nodded his head slowly from side to side.

"None of them are capable of simple belief in anything. If they were, they wouldn't be here."

Meantime another clergyman had begun to speak.

"I thoroughly agree with Professor Dendrane," he was saying. "I too spent my life in educational work and I know how to put the Christian message across to the young..."

I leaned back again to whisper to Lamiel.

"Were none of these clergy ordinary parish priests?"

"Very few of them. In most cases they were canons, administrative officials, teachers and college chaplains."

"It is unfortunate that they are the people on earth

who tend to be regarded as the Church's chief spokes-men."

"Unfortunate," agreed Lamiel, "but inevitable. Earnest parish priests are too busy with pastoral work to be able to assume the Voice of the Church in the press and in public meetings. And, oddly enough, most of them imagine that they are too unlearned for that kind of thing. Their humility preserves them from the public forum. You will find that the present company are not much impeded by that particular obstacle to utterance."

I resumed my attention to the educational clergy-man.

"Science, politics, education and welfare have failed to bring men happiness and they have failed to bring the world prosperity. That has always been my theme. Try the Sermon on the Mount. Try Christian Charity. Here is an old yet new recipe for personal happiness and social well-being. This is better than ar-maments, better than socialism, better than govern-ment controls. I have preached this Christian message a thousand times. Christian Love opens the door to abundant personal living. Christian Love is the key to prosperity and peace."

There was some applause for this declaration; but a number of the more sensitive members of the audience shook their heads disdainfully, as though the appeal did not quite come up to their intellectual level. After looking round the room, the chairman now rose again to draw the meeting to a close.

"It is good," he said, "that our deliberations should end on this harmonious note. We have reason to be proud that the dignity of our institution is matched by the friendliness of our discussions. If only Christians below had learned the secret of that true charity which permeates our common life in this revered, this beloved college. In the bond of brotherhood let us end our..."

"No, no, no!" There was a sudden excited cry from the back of the room. A slight, nervous-looking fellow had jumped to his feet. His voice and his hands trembled as he spoke. "If you please...I should like to say something...I must say it....Of course, I appreciate what has been said by others...but I've begun to wonder whether perhaps we are, all of us, rather missing the point...."

A dead silence descended upon the hall and a look of discomfiture appeared on the chairman's face. The nervous man continued rapidly and jerkily.

"It has occurred to me, as I listened, that perhaps we've got hold of the wrong end of the stick—I mean, in talking about the need to continue searching for truth, and in being disappointed that we find nothing here to help us. It's just an odd thought I've had—silly, perhaps, but there may be something in it. I mean, is it that we are at fault ourselves? Are we making the wrong approach?"

A low murmur of disapproval was heard at this point and one or two people laughed.

"What I'm trying to say is this. Are we perhaps missing something that is really here if we knew how to look for it?"

The laughter now became general; but the nervous man was not dismayed. Indeed he seemed to gain in confidence.

"I don't think you understand what I'm trying to say. I mean, have we perhaps missed something by relying always on ourselves to get us there? And are we

missing something now because we refuse to recognize
what there is about us? It all sounds complicated, I
know: but really it just amounts to this. Ought we distrust ourselves a little more than we do? Suppose we
were to ask for someone to come and instruct us?"

The laughter was increasing all the time in volume,
and the speaker's last words provoked an uproarious
thunder of jocularity. It was some moments before the
chairman could make himself heard above the noise,
and it was quite impossible for the nervous man to add
anything further. As soon as the chairman gained a
hearing, he announced the end of the meeting, where-
upon the laughter began again. The room was alive
with it as members began to file to get into the corridor. We were walking across the quadrangle when
someone drew close and put his hand on Lamiel's
arm. It was the nervous-looking man whose contribution had caused the turmoil.

"Excuse me," he said, "but I think you can help
me."

"I'm sure I can," said Lamiel reassuringly.

"I was perfectly happy here at first," the man went
on. "I liked the company. I felt that these people knew
all the answers. But somehow I've come to feel that
we're not really getting anywhere. I don't want to be
continually told what I know already: I want to be
told what I don't know. There's no use in standing
still. And today, during the speeches, I began to feel
that perhaps we're not even standing still: perhaps
we're going backwards, as it were. It can't be right to
progress here further and further into scepticism—to
begin to whittle away what little faith we began with.
There wouldn't be any sense in the whole setup, if that
were what it was meant to do to us. That's the root of

my difficulties. I've always had the feeling that there *must* be sense in things, if you see what I mean."

"I see perfectly," said Lamiel.

"I'm afraid I made a bit of a fool of myself in there. I don't express myself very well. I'm not like most of the others. My background was different. I didn't have the advantage of a Public School education."

"You didn't have a Public School education," said Lamiel. "That would be a better way of putting it."

"And now I'm anxious to learn; yet I don't feel that I'm making headway. Can you help me to someone who might take me in hand?"

"I certainly can. I may say that I am glad you feel as you do. It is right that you should. You must come with us."

"I shall be delighted."

The fellow looked comforted: he was visibly more at ease. As we reached the Porter's Lodge and escaped the press of numbers, Lamiel began to question our new acquaintance, pausing as he did so.

"What is your name?" he asked quietly.

"Oliver Milnthorpe."

I felt it discreet to withdraw a few paces whilst they talked, and I began idly to examine the notices displayed on the wall.

CHRISTIAN DOCTRINE: ITS RELEVANCE HERE
AND NOW

by Rev. R. Froward, M.A., Ph.D. (London), formerly Secretary of the Council for the Diffusion of Discreet Interdenominationalism.

JOURNEY THROUGH THE GRAVE
A Symposium

Members recall their experience and review their beliefs in the light of what it has taught them.

NECROSOPHICAL STUDY GROUP

Contact with local inhabitants has revealed the prevalence here of superstitions generally discarded on earth.

It is proposed to form a committee to examine ways of presenting a rational faith to Heliconians.

IS CHRISTIANITY NECESSARILY THEISTIC?

A friendly discussion between two members who hold different views upon this subject.

For the pro-theistic school: Professor Dendrane, D.D.

For the post-theistic school: Rev. S. Goodenough, B.Sc. (Econ.), formerly chaplain of CARCHESTER COLLEGE.

The place was obviously alive with intellectual activity. Notice after notice advertised lectures, discussions, brainstrusts, seminars and study groups. It was hard to find a notice of any other kind but, after a quick survey of the whole board, I did at last light upon a single one. It read thus:

MORNING PRAYERS

At a meeting of the Members' Union Committee, it was unanimously decided to abandon for the present the daily meeting for morning prayers in the Hall at ten o'clock.

As I studied this in some surprise, a person came and stood at my side. I pointed to the notice and turned to question him.

"Why were the prayers abandoned."

"Oh, for many reasons," he said. "Members felt that they were no longer meeting a real need. You see, the canons have their daily services in the minster and are fully catered for. We others, less formally committed to institutional religion, are trying to discover the truth for ourselves. We are pursuing many very different lines of thought, and most of us have reservations about this or that doctrinal implication in the formal liturgical prayers. In fact, we found it impossible to frame prayers which offended no one. It would be dishonest to join in prayers worded in such a way that we could not give assent to them. We are determined to avoid hypocrisy of that kind. So we are omitting public prayers until such time as we manage to arrive, by our studies, at some clearly formulable beliefs which are generally acceptable. This may prove a difficult task; but it is the only honest thing to do."

I was denied further information on this matter, for Lamiel touched me on the shoulder.

"Come," he said. "You have seen what there is to see."

The three of us left the college, descended the steps and turned into the street.

5

We had not walked far when Lamiel exclaimed, "Here he comes! I did not think we should have long to wait."

An angel was approaching us who, when he came up, greeted us as though he had expected to meet us.

"I understand that Oliver is ready for my guardianship again."

He saluted us with upraised hand as he spoke. Oliver and I bowed, while Lamiel returned his salutation, saying, "I think you will find that he is fully prepared for guardianship. A very brief stay with the gnostics seems to have done the trick. How was it that he came to be among them?"

"A fairly typical case," said Oliver's Guardian. "He was not in contact with our people during the years of young manhood, but a few scraps of scriptural instruction at school had left him with the suspicion that there might be something in religion. He began to want to know a few things about it. Unfortunately, instead of going to Church or asking his parish priest for instruction, he started attending Evening Classes in the study of Comparative Religion. It might have cost him everything, as you can well imagine; but he has been treated very generously here. We had to take into account his very deficient upbringing. The parents were not a great help. He didn't have many opportunities. And then the victims of Adult Education—the really well-meaning victims, that is—always win our especial sympathy. The Devil has such a hold on that work; and he doesn't quite play fair. You've got to treat the rules of the game pretty loosely when your opponent is breaking them right and left. So there was every reason for giving Oliver a chance. I'm glad it has worked."

Oliver looked slightly bewildered during this conversation, but it was a happy kind of bewilderment. There was no sign of suspicion or dismay in his eyes, as Lamiel committed him to his Guardian's care, and we went our separate ways with a sense of relief.

I was now able to put to Lamiel a question which I was impatient to have answered.

"How often do defections of this kind from the College for Gnostics occur?"

"Two or three in a good month," said Lamiel.

"And what happens to the others? Do they just stay there?"

"Yes. They continue their studies in their own way."

"Forever?"

"Oh, dear no. Not forever."

"Then do they die—I mean, really die?"

"*Death* is not quite the right word for what happens. I think the word *breakdown* would convey the idea to you most effectively. The reason gives way—I mean the whole reason; not just the capacity for ratiocination, but the whole power of apprehending the objective order. The intellect ceases to find external nourishment and the will atrophies through lack of exercise. There is no faith to sustain these faculties. It is a very gradual process, and eventually the victim ceases to believe even in the existence of his fellow-members. He becomes a great nuisance, sometimes knocking them down and walking over them. Then we have to remove him."

"Where to?"

"To the Infirmary."

"And then?"

"It is not for us to enquire. The doors close upon him. There is nothing then but the Divine Mercy."

I was silent for a few moments and then I spoke again, rather apologetically.

"I hope you don't mind my questions about these people. I am very interested in what happens to them."

"You have good reason to be," said Lamiel coldly. "I quite understand your sympathy for them."

"Well, isn't it a little hard to leave them utterly to themselves? Isn't it possible to send someone to instruct them?"

"Even against their will? It would be quite useless. You can instruct only those who seek instruction. Surely you have not spent a lifetime in education without knowing the difference between the teachable and the unteachable? And, in any case, is it instruction that they really need? In fact, it is not."

"But surely there is some inconsistency here. Oliver was removed as soon as he began to ask for instruction; yet you say that instruction is not what the members of the college need."

Lamiel smiled indulgently.

"I'm afraid you are very obtuse," he said. "I am continually surprised by the extent of your dullness. The members of the college certainly need to reach the stage of feeling that they need to be instructed. But that does not mean that, in fact, instruction is what they require—unless you use the word *instruction* very loosely. It is faith that they require. The sense of needing instruction is the germ of faith. But of course, actual instruction—intellectual fodder, if you like—merely feeds their self-reliance, so that they do not sense their own inadequacy, their own need for instruction. Suppose we sent members of the Hierarchy on an organized teaching mission to them. And suppose we managed to convey to them the proposition that self-dominated intellectualism is a snare. They would feast their intellects so gluttonously upon this new proposition that their state would be worse than ever. They would be even less likely to arrive at that sense of inadequacy—to realize their need for instruction. Don't you see that the only thing to do is to leave them to themselves? Left to themselves, they are at least deprived of new propositions. For new propositions are arrived at only by scholars who are humbly waiting upon revelation. There are no such scholars in the College for Gnostics. We cut them off; we give them the chance to awaken to the staleness of their arid, uncreative intellectualism. And, as a result, we gain a few defections, as you have heard."

"It is very complicated," I said.

"Of course it is. Evil is always complicated. Truth is simple; but truth is found only by faith."

"And is there then no way of waking them to faith?"

"What do you mean?" asked Lamiel.

"Well, couldn't they be moved by some clear revelation?"

"Some carefully staged miracle? You've asked that question before in a different form. The answer is still the same. We can't coerce these people into faith. A little question of freedom is involved. Confusing, no doubt, here as down below; but there it is, and we have to accept it. If it were possible to coerce into faith, then faith would no longer be faith. Moreover our whole organization would be pointless. Existence would be tedious, to say the least. Quite frankly, I can't imagine how we could occupy ourselves. There'd be nothing to do."

"But you speak as though these men were utterly unacquainted with the Christian Faith. They are not pagans. They have learned a lot about the Christian Gospel."

"Collectively," said Lamiel, "they have learned everything about it, except what matters most. Christians who have not come to self-committal are Christians who have not attained to faith. And Christians who have not attained to faith can be called Christian only by courtesy. Our friends in the College are sufficiently informed to tell you that. In Helicon the talk is all of moral endeavour and courageous pursuit of truth; they speak of the illumination vouchsafed by the Eternal Wisdom to those who claim in Christianity nothing more than the best working hypothesis. You have heard language different from this on the lips of God's priests and teachers below. You have heard of repentance and self-surrender, of the grace of Redemption, and of regeneration in the living power of the Resurrection. You have heard too of the Mystical Body of baptized believers, nourished in the spirit by word and sacrament. Of course, these things too may be assimilated by the intellect without being absorbed into the personality and greeted by the will. The intellect of one man may feed in self-centerdness upon these doctrines, whilst his neighbour's intellect feeds upon systematized permutations for the Football Pools: and yet the two men may be in the same spiritual condition. The darkest possibility of all is that one may *know* even all this that I now say to you, and yet *only know* it. You admit that this is a very dark possibility?"

He turned and looked at me, but I avoided his eyes. I was glad that we were walking, so that I could evade the penetrating gaze without discourtesy.

"Yes," I said, "it is a possibility, and it is a dark one." We walked a few paces further in silence before I added, "And that, I suppose, is why I'm being shown this place."

"That is why you are here."

I looked around. We had walked through the square and back again up the main street of Helicon. We had passed on the left the end of the little lane from the minster by which we had come. I had turned to look down it and had seen the knoll of trees and the towers of the minster beyond. From that point we had continued for about a quarter for a mile, climbing slightly all the time. And now we made our way through the ancient city gate. Judging from the position of the minster, it must be the West Gate, I decided. And probably the gate by which we had originally entered Helicon was the South Gate;

though we had turned to left and to right so many times between the gate and the minster that it was difficult to be certain about it. In any case, all this reasoning rested on two unconfined suppositions: the first that the minster pointed to the East and had its twin towers at the West end; the second, that North, South, East and West meant here what they meant on earth. If they did, then the valley in which Lamiel and I had met Squash ran from East to West. The sun had been directly behind me when I sat on the bank, and it must have been near midday. Since then we had crossed the stream, had turned northwestwards along the ridge of the widening valley, and had swung round so as to enter the city from the South.

My geographical calculations preoccupied me so that I took little notice of my surroundings for some time. When I again looked around me, I saw that we had left behind us the houses which clustered around the outside of the city walls. The road had become narrower and there were more trees. As we forked right into a rough cart-track, Lamiel read my thoughts.

"You want to know where we are going?"

"Yes," I said, hesitantly, trying not to be too curious.

"We are about to call upon an old acquaintance of yours. It would not be right to leave this district without looking him up. You remember Tony Riddell?"

"I remember him well enough. We were good friends at Oxford."

"But you drifted apart."

"It is only natural," I said. "One develops new interests. Our ways diverged."

"And your thoughts too."

"Yes; we came to look at things very differently."

"He despised you as the victim of superstitious dogmatism."

"I shouldn't put it as strongly as that. He liked to be free and unfettered in his thinking: he hated to accept opinions at second-hand: but I'm sure he respected my point of view."

"He didn't respect it. Nor did you respect his. Secretly you both despised each other's intellectual position. It was a pity. You might have done each other a lot of good. There was a purpose in your relationship; and it was not served."

All this made me feel very uncomfortable, and I tried to change the course of the conversation.

"I shouldn't have expected to find Tony among the gnostics," I said.

"He isn't. He is well outside the city; well outside any city. That has a significance which you will understand later. We shall find him at the bottom of this hill."

We had ceased to climb and now we began a gradual descent into a wide valley, sprinkled with farms, cottages and barns. The sun was sinking behind the hills ahead of us and the whole scene had a mellow appearance. Here at last was the idyllic rural setting imagined in earthly dreams of paradisal peace. How Tony would revel in it! He had always posed as the incurable romantic—the boy who never grew up. This I had eventually found irritating. The romanticism of nineteen rests uncomfortably on the personality at thirty-five. There was a time when I enjoyed Tony's declarations about the religious sacredness of youth's sexual desires and his poetic raptures about primitive man's divine inheritance of unspoiled nature and un-corrupted passion. But the time came when I wearied of his interest in sexuality and Nature-Worship; and I was ready to talk about something else. Unfortunately Tony never reached the stage of being willing to talk about anything else at all. Instead of growing out of this, he grew into it more and more. He took to spending his summer holidays in a Nudist Camp, and began to dilate upon the hypocrisy and obscenity of wearing clothes in July. It was at one of these camps that he met the girl he was to marry. There is something distinctly embarrassing about a man who first introduces you to his fiancée by displaying a nude photograph. I felt that his obsession had become unheathly.

The worst thing was that it masqueraded as a religion. "God is Love," Tony would say in explanation, and nobody had ever told him about *agape* and *eros*. Not that he needed to be told much about *eros*. I got weary of the crude pantheism and the pseudo-mystical sexuality, and suggested one day that perhaps coition was not the only sacrament. He smiled patronizingly and I felt that the gap between us was further widened.

"Here we are," said Lamiel, stopping at the gate of a cottage, which had everything right about it from the thatched roof to the roses round the door. "I think we shall find him at home."

We were received by a bewildered, almost dazed Tony, who seated us around a log fire in a very "ye-olde" sitting room. As I stared at the pewter tankards, copper warming-pans and wrought-iron candlesticks, I began to feel the conversation was going to be difficult. For one thing, Tony did not look at us, and the vague, searching expression in his eyes suggested that he was not even fully aware of our presence.

"You are working on the land?" said Lamiel, leaning forward as if anxious to catch his attention.

"Land or sea; it is all the same," said Tony dreamily. "I serve daily the great sweet Mother—mother and lover of men. Out of her the years roll. At eventide she bids me rest. The ploughman homeward treads his weary way, and I return to my lowly cot."

This sounded too unbearably stilted to be serious. It was as though Tony were caricaturing himself in some diabolically perverse fashion. I was on the point of laughing, when I caught the fervent look in his eyes.

"Don't you find it lonely here?" I ventured.

"I am never alone. Mimi lives ever in my heart. There is God in the garden in the cool of the evening. And beyond there is always the sky—and the trees."

"Quite so," said Lamiel.

"There is society where none intrudes," Tony went on. "God made the country; but man made the town. I was always content to commune with myself and with the silent hills."

"I wonder you don't find the communion a little one-sided," said Lamiel.

"All I ask is the heaven above and the road before me."

"There is some confusion, I think," said Lamiel, "between two lyrics, both justly popular with the anthologists."

For my part I felt there was even greater confusion between the two present speakers. They didn't seem to be making contact at all. I tried to do something about it.

"Tony," I said, "Lamiel is my Guardian. He has been a great help to me..."

"Thank you," said Lamiel heavily; but I went on shamelessly.

"I'm sure he could help you, Tony."

Then Tony's face suddenly changed. For the first time he turned and actually looked at us.

"So you've brought along somebody to convert me, have you!" he sneered. "Keep your Trinity and your original sin to yourself."

"These things are not under dispute," Lamiel said coldly.

"I've heard it all," Tony shouted. "You smear the loveliest things of life with your vulgar obscenities. Your God is the Husband and Son of a Virgin. A virgin! What a filthy defilement of sacred things; to regard the union of man and woman as too impure for divinity to share. The indecency of it; the dirt; the prurience!"

This was a bitter moment; but it was a moment of real contact, when Tony looked us both in the eyes. Unfortunately it didn't last. We just couldn't build upon it. The dreamy, faraway look returned to Tony's eyes and the language of the Quiet Corner came again to his lips. He chanted calmly into the distance, "My God is the God of the lambkin and the daffadowndilly; the God who lit the flame of desire in Mimi's eyes. The loveliest things of beauty God ever has shown to me—are her voice and her hair and her thighs, and the dear white curve of her hips."

"You don't improve the text by your ingenious emendations," said Lamiel, and then added more quietly, "I don't think there's anything to be done."

I didn't understand at all. I only saw that Tony was out of touch. He had always been keen on amateur theatricals. I should have liked to believe that this burlesque of his own character was a comic performance. I looked for some sudden revealing burst of laughter from him—some crisp leap from bathos to wit. But it didn't come.

"Do you enjoy your work?" I asked, making yet another attempt to communicate.

"I till the blessed earth, loving the God who made me. I plunge the spade and wield the sickle, and every act is a prayer."

"A prayer for what?" asked Lamiel.

"For what we are about to receive," said Tony, "take the thanks of a boy!"

He stared absently into the fire. I knew for certain now that he was not fully conscious of our presence, except in fitful flashes too brief for sustained communication. And I doubted whether he had realized my identity at all.

"Tony," I said earnestly. "You remember me: you remember Oxford."

It was not a happy choice of opening. I could see that Lamiel disapproved of my contribution, and I soon knew why. For the situation grew worse. Tony lifted up his head as if to preach to a vast audience.

"Lovely all times she lies," he chanted, "lovely tonight. I have kept faith: I have kept faith. I have not felt the lapse of hours. One aim, one business, one desire. One God and Father of us all, who loves us all. One hope, one glory..."

"You might add," said Lamiel, "one Lord, one Faith, one Baptism."

"And one far-off divine event," said Tony, his voice rising as if for some magnificent peroration, "to which the whole creation moves...

So will I build my altar in the fields,
And the blue sky my fretted dome shall be,
And the sweet fragrance that the wild flower yields
Shall be the incense I will yield to Thee—

Thee, Mimi, my only love. Forever and ever mine!"

"I think," said Lamiel, "that we might as well go."

6

We slept that night in a barn not far from Tony's cottage—or rather *I* slept in a barn; Lamiel did not seem to need sleep. And in the morning we followed the track across the wide valley until, swinging round to the left, it rejoined the road by which we had left Helicon. This road had itself become now a mere track, very narrow, and to all appearances little used. We followed it in a westerly direction until it ran, at right angles, slap into a great highway running North and South. We turned South along this highway and I saw how it ran straight as a die for as far as the eye could see. I felt now that my previous geographical conjectures were confirmed. We were destined for Fordshaw. Now, in the valley south of Helicon, Lamiel had told Squash and Mrs. Templecombe to cross the East-West ridge on the southern side, and then to bear right when they ran into the track. This track, according to Lamiel, joined the main road to Fordshaw. It seemed likely that this was the same main road and that we were joining it at a point further North. But why did this great highway skirt the city of Helicon? And why were all the approaches to the city either

narrow lanes or rough tracks? I began to modify my
estimate of Helicon. Plainly it was a less important
place than it had appeared to be. There was no proper
approach to it across that wild valley to the South. Lamiel and I, approaching Helicon from the Southwest,
Squash and Mrs. Templecombe, leaving for the South-
east—we had all found ourselves descending and
climbing pathless banks and scrambling over an un-
bridged stream. Did not the importance of the place
justify better travelling facilities than this? The question struck me the more forcibly on account of the in-
congruity between the ancient and massive city gates,
which had impressed me with the dignity of the place,
and the narrowness and roughness of the lanes leading
up to them. I had seen two of these gateways, both noble and impressive structures, yet I now knew that, in
each case, the road leading outwards rapidly de-
generated into a narrow country lane and then into a
rough track. And now this great highway, missing the
city completely, brought the contrast home more forcibly still.

"Helicon is not exactly at the hub of the universe," I
said to Lamiel.

"You have half-formed the opinion," said Lamiel,
"that Helicon is an unimportant city. At the same time
you suspect that an opinion formed on superficial appearances may be wrong. You are anxious to have your
opinion confirmed, and at the same time you are anxious to avoid appearing stupid. You therefore take ref-
uge in a facetious and tentative utterance, oddly
compounded of litotes and hyperbole. It would be
better to ask a plain, straightforward question. Nevertheless the cautious desire not to put your foot in it, as
they say, is not entirely blameworthy."

Lamiel could be particularly exasperating when he talked like this. I felt justified in pointing out how irritating it could be.

"When a university don subjects one's philosophical generalizations to this kind of analysis, the result is often illuminating. But isn't it rather heavy-handed to treat a simple conversational statement to this devastating analytical dissection?"

"The statement in question may well deserve to be called conversational," said Lamiel. "The art of conversation has been so perverted of late below, that perhaps your inexact utterance may be regarded as a fair specimen of the art. But I cannot agree that the statement was simple. On the contrary, as I have shown, it was a peculiarly complex device for avoiding the simplicity of a direct question or of a clear expression of opinion."

"Very well, then," I said, "but does it matter?"

"Of course it matters. We have talked of the virtue of self-committal. Do you think you can even begin to learn self-committal in the gravest moral and spiritual matters, if you are yet incapable, in lesser matters, of committing yourself to simple questions or simple expressions of opinion? Was there not an enormous evasion in saying, 'Helicon is not exactly at the hub of the universe'?"

"The figure of speech is so familiar that no one but a logical positivist would jib at it."

Lamiel waved his hand in deprecation.

"Oh, dear, how you misunderstand me. Or rather, how you pretend to misunderstand me. I am not so unscientific as to have any literalist prejudices against metaphor. I am not putting the stupid question—Did you mean 'hub' when you said 'hub,' or 'universe' when you said 'universe'? I am criticizing you because you withdrew yourself from your own statement even in the act of uttering it. You did not dare to commit yourself."

"Very well, then," I said. "Is Helicon an important city?"

"You will admit that, put like that, the question sounds silly. The silliness was there all the time, of course; but I have persuaded you to bring it to light."

"Because I don't really know what I mean by 'important.'"

"Exactly. Because you could introduce only earthly notions of importance which have little relevance here. If you reflect carefully, instead of blurting out nonsense, you will realize that your question is already answered. Do the members of the College for Gnostics think they are weightily involved in things that matter? Of course they do. Are they getting anywhere? No, they are not. Oliver's case has shown that they begin to get somewhere only when they realize that they are getting nowhere. And at that point they are removed from Helicon. Very well, then; that answers the real question. But you are concerned about something else, too. You are looking for some crude allegorical significance in the fact that Helicon is an isolated city which the main highways do not touch. This is again to miss the point. There are no allegorical significances here. Things do not stand for other things in that symbolic way. Things are what they are. Helicon, noble in architecture, venerable in atmosphere, restless in intellectual enquiry, is quite simple and unallegorically off the beaten track. I'm afraid you will find Fordshaw very different."

I did find Fordshaw very different. When we entered the city, some hours later, I felt, in some horribly perverted kind of way, as though I had come home. Down on earth I had known cities of considerable size, with huge industrial populations, which had become cities of importance only during the last hundred years. Previously they were mere hamlets and, in some cases, not even that. In such cities it is almost impossible to find a building dating back beyond the mid-nineteenth century. If he is accustomed to an environment littered with ancient buildings and reeking with historical associations, the visitor is inevitably depressed by a sense of rootlessness in cities of this kind. Now here in Fordshaw I was overcome immediately by just such a feeling of rootlessness; and, as I gradually saw more and more of the place, I began to understand why. For there did not seem to be a single building which could be said to date back beyond the First World War. Judging by the architectural fashions I was accustomed to, I was compelled to believe that the whole place was less than forty years old. I remarked on this to Lamiel.

"Your notions of time," he said, "make it difficult for me to explain to you. You are quite right to say that the place is new. It always has been. That is to say—if you can understand my meaning—it has been very new for a very long time."

"That sounds like a contradiction to me."

"Yes, it is bound to. But suppose we put it like this. There is a considerable labour force here, and they are continually rebuilding the place."

"Is that necessary?"

"Not at all. It is not a matter merely of replacing crumbling fabrics. It's just that they don't like anything old, and the fashions of the period immediately preceding their own are particularly abhorrent to them."

"By their own period, I suppose you mean the period which was theirs on earth."

"Yes. They have recently had a great drive to get rid of the last vestiges of late nineteenth-century building. And I think you'll agree that they've done the job pretty thoroughly."

It was certainly true. Factories, shops, houses were all in the newest styles. And Fordshaw was different from Helicon in being full of shops. Moreover there were cars, lorries and buses in the streets, and plenty of garages. Just now we were passing a huge petrol station on our left, with a row of blue petrol pumps labelled "SHEX," and beside them a row of scarlet pumps labelled "ESTO." Along the roof of the garage ran posters advertising the petrol—

SHEX IS EXCELLENT. SEE PARADISE WITHOUT PINKING

and

ESTO—THE SPIRIT THAT GIVETH LIFE

The sight of this petrol station satisfied my curiosity, for I had already seen numerous posters which had confused me. One was the bare legend—

ESTO GIVES YOU THE GODSPEED THROUGH
PURGATORY

Another had been even more bewildering. There was a huge picture of a man driving a motorbike at a furious speed. Behind him an angel was falling off backwards from his seat on the pillion. The caption screamed in startling letters—

SHAKE HIM OFF WITH SHEX!

Other advertisements at the garage were of the same kind. A picture of a man approaching his car, jug in hand, with a face contorted in imbecilic laughter, was captioned—

ANOINT IT WITH GLUSOL: THE OIL OF GLADNESS

which explained an unillustrated slogan nearby—

OTHERS PARTLY MISS: BUT GLUSOL WHOLLY OILS

A row of shops just beyond the garage produced even more startling advertisements, not dissimilar in tone. There was a huge store with several windows devoted to ladies' clothing. The trade name was apparently "DOLORES," for it appeared everywhere. Repeated several times was a remarkable jingle—

> This highly exclusive store is
> Devoted to feminine glories.
> Come in, and consult Dolores,
> Our Lady of Tone.

In one window a smartly costumed wax figure held a notice proclaiming—

I GIVE THANKS TO DOLORES: SHE HAS FASHIONED ME
BEHIND AND BEFORE

In another window, full of lingerie, a huge corset clung tight around an artifical section of a torso. The thing as a whole extended only from the waist to the thighs, and had a grotesque appearance, being supported on a single wooden pole. Above it one could read—

LET DOLORES FIT YOU: FOR SHE KNOWETH YOUR
DOWNSITTINGS AND YOUR UPRISINGS

In a third window a chain of linked articles, designed for the support of the female figure, garlanded a placard in the same vein—

LET DOLORES FIT YOU: FOR SHE KNOWETH
WHEREOF YOU ARE MADE

Staring into this window, I suddenly became conscious of Lamiel's disapproval, and I hastily turned to look across the street to our right. There was a cinema, called "THE BEATIFIC," advertising a film with the title "GUARDIAN OF MY HEART." A poster showed a young woman kneeling at the feet of an angel, and looking up at him with pleading, sentimental gaze. The angel stood looking into the distance, as if firmly repressing some impulse of tenderness. The thing was astonishingly vulgar, and I said so; but Lamiel only nodded and looked straight ahead, as if in silent distaste of his surroundings. And indeed the outward appearance of the city seemed to caricature the most unworthy features of modern civilization down below. Every other shop seemed to be either a fashion shop or a newsagent's; and papers were stacked in great piles on the stalls. I could read their names as we passed— "THE CELESTIAL ECHO," "THE FORDSHAW ADVERTISER," "THE ETERNAL RECORD," "PARADISAL POST," and so on.

I was fascinated by much that I saw, and I should

dearly have liked to linger and feast on the shop windows and advertisements, which offered such odd correspondences with what I had known below. A bus station especially interested me, for it advertised a Sunday Excursion to Helicon:

See this charming old-world city, no longer inaccessible. Special arrangements for transport from the highway to the city gates.

But this, and so much more, was quickly left behind, as Lamiel strode on with unusual determination. Indeed, whenever anything especially whetted my appetite, he seemed to quicken his pace for the very purpose of forestalling delay. Only once did I induce him to stop and allow me to study a shop window. It was a kind of chemist's shop, full of bottles, packets, little boxes and the like. The remedies advertised seemed to be entirely for nervous and mental complaints:

Are you subject to attacks of REMORSE?
Try ZEST-VITE.
Restores you to self-confident living!

Do not wake at night to memories of sin.
HARTLICK'S cures NIGHT-REPENTANCE!

Burdlipp's Sedative for Biting Consciences.

CALLOUS WILL TONIC keeps the Contrition Germ at bay!

BANISH GUILT-NEUROSIS

Prevention is better than Cure
Nip *Penititis* in the bud
At the first lump in the throat, Suck a SINSTOP
For *Penititis* of the head, Suck a SINSTOP
For *Penititis* of the heart, Suck a SINSTOP
Everybody's saying it: Everybody's doing it:
GO SUCK A SINSTOP!

"It's decadent," I said, as we stood surveying the contents of the window.

"It is bad," agreed Lamiel. "But there is one thing worse than going to buy a pack of Sinstops."

"Well?" I asked, apprehensive of the customary personal challenge—and I was not to be disappointed.

"This is worse—looking in the window without feeling even the slightest need of a Sinstop. Come along. It is not illuminating."

We walked on.

"I allowed you to look into that window," Lamiel added a few moments later, "because I thought the sight might benefit you. Do not be content with a superficial judgment upon things. The advertisements there make an appeal to evil escapism, it is true; but the existence of the pills and potions proves that there is a prevailing tendency towards self-criticism, which has to be combated."

"I hadn't thought of that."

"No. Yet the point must not be overlooked. I am only anxious that you should see straight. Do not allow your judgments to be clouded and confused by the mere influence of vulgarity. We saw no chemist's shops of this kind in the refined streets of Helicon. Is Helicon any the better for that? It may be quite the reverse. Did you meet in Helicon any prevailing tendency to-

wards self-criticism, which the advertisers of these potions might have appealed to?"

"No," I said. "I can see that there would be no trade
in Helicon for them."

"Exactly. This enables us to reason in a clear-
headed manner. Helicon has no vulgarity comparable
to the vulgarity of the chemist's shop; but we must not
be deluded by refinement and respectability. Helicon
is also comfortably free, to all appearances, of residents suffering from Guilt-Neurosis, the Contrition
Germ, Night-Repentance and Penititis."

Lamiel had spoken none too soon. For of course I
had been inwardly comparing the vulgarity of Fordshaw with the quiet refinement of Helicon; and I had
certainly allowed this comparison to establish in my
mind the idea that Fordshaw was by far the more evil
of the two places. I now saw my error. Helicon was the
more attractive of the two cities to anyone sensitive to
twentieth-century barbarism; but for that very reason
it was perhaps more dangerous. The blaring restless-
ness of Fordshaw was an incitement to seek a more
blessed city. The smug respectability of Helicon might
more easily ensnare the soul.

"Here," said Lamiel, "is another vulgarity unknown
to Helicon. Yet I doubt whether Helicon is any the
better for that."

He pointed across the road to a series of WAYSIDE
PULPIT placards, and his pace slackened, as if he
wished me to ponder them. I read the first one
aloud—

GOD IS KNOCKING AT THE DOOR OF YOUR HEART
OPEN AND LET HIM IN

"The Divine Challenge comes to every man," said Lamiel, "but one is not happy to see the Omnipotent and All-Glorious imagined as a postman."

I read the next—

GIVE A LAME DOG A HELPING HAND—
YOUR CHRISTIAN DEED FOR TODAY

"A single act of charity to one in distress," said Lamiel, "whether man or beast, is always worth performing; but it is doubtful whether its performance ought to leave the Christian with the conviction that he has fulfilled his religious obligations for the next twenty-four hours."

A SONG IN THE HEART EASES LIFE'S DAILY BURDEN

"That is better," said Lamiel, "for its claims are less comprehensive, and it makes no pretence to be a specifically Christian exhortation. Of course, the literalist might question the efficacy of inward music as an antidote against the more sordid aspects of industrial toil."

"There is one more," I said—

"COUNT YOUR BLESSINGS THEN YOU WILL KNOW
CONTENTMENT"

Lamiel paused a moment this time, and then said, "There is a school of thought which condemns such exhortations as misleading. It may be claimed that the practice of enumerating good things received at the hand of Providence tends rather towards self-satisfaction than towards self-surrender. It is not the business of the Church to nourish complacency....But I think we are getting near our destination."

He stopped as we came up against a crossroads, so busy and imposing that I judged it to be the heart of the city. The road which now ran to our left and right was plainly the main street. It was wide enough to take six streams of traffic abreast; and on either side buildings of five stories and upwards rose above the shop windows. Lamiel paused for a moment, looking first to right, then to left.

"Are you not sure of the way?" I asked.

"This is the street we are seeking. I was just wondering in which direction the Institute lies. I have been there before; but I am glad to say that I have not had cause to visit Fordshaw recently....Ah, yes. We go to the right."

"*Fordshaw* is an odd name," I said, as we began to walk again.

"Yes, and you will find some odd theories about it among the local inhabitants. It was originally called Fordshaw for the very obvious reason that the river was fordable here—the place of the ford. I think you are philologist enough to understand that. Such, however, is the ignorance here of history and historical studies, and such is the passion for novelty, that a fanciful etymological theory has lately become popular. It is being said that the city is named after two prominent twentieth-century figures; the one an industrial magnate, who contributed something to the development of mass-production techniques; the other a writer of plays, who veiled a remarkable confusion of thought in a specious clarity of utterance. His outspokenness gained him considerable notoriety, I believe, though it was often difficult for the rational mind to know whither his outspokenness tended. But these names probably mean more to you than they do to me. Be that as it may, two days have been set aside in honour of these gentlemen, who are being cultivated as patrons of the city. Some are declaring them the city's founders."

Lamiel now stopped before a massive square red brick building on our right. Rows of identical windows reached out into the distance. The concrete roof was flat, and the whole place had a dismal, factory like appearance.

"This is it," he said. "It suffers from a defect peculiar to twentieth-century architecture. You can never tell, from looking at the thing as a whole, where you are likely to find the main entrance."

We walked on a little and eventually came upon an unimpressive flight of half-a-dozen steps, with two swing doors at the top. A notice over the doors read—

I.T.T.T. (Fordshaw)
INSTITUTE OF TENTATIVE THEOLOGICAL
TECHNOLOGY

"We always call it the 'Backward Believers' Department,' " said Lamiel, "and that of course is its proper name. But I suppose it was scarcely to be expected that the members would keep the name, for they were given control of the place. The same treatment is given here as at Helicon in that respect. Let us go in."

We entered and, after Lamiel had studied a board in the vestibule, which gave some account of the various offices and halls in the building, we took a lift up to the top floor, and eventually made our way to a door labelled "The Director." Lamiel knocked and we went in.

A timid-looking man sat behind a desk. His fair hair

was thinned away to baldness at the front of the head, but still quite thick at the back. He had a pale, slightly angular face, and two furtive eyes which darted about, as he spoke, in all directions, as though they belonged to an animal caught in a trap.

"Good morning," he said, and an extraordinary, unconvincing smile flashed on and off. This smile was so brief as to be almost indistinguishable from a screwing-up of the face expressive of pain. It punctuated all his utterances. One felt that it was worked by a switch, so automatic was it in appearance. "Do sit down. I was told to expect you."

I sat down, but Lamiel, as usual, remained standing.

"My ward here is interested in the name you have given to this institute, Dr. Primrose."

"Yes, yes, of course," said the director, flashing the smile on and off for each of us in turn. "It is...er...well...er...we don't like to be too explicit ...there's such a lot we don't know, isn't there?...One has to be careful. Theological conclusions are only tentative, aren't they? We mustn't make the mistake of the bigots in the past, claiming for certainties things which are quite beyond the grasp of human minds....We like to make it felt that we know the limitations....We are all in the dark, in a manner of speaking....We haven't got the proofs which so much strengthen the position of the scientists. And we must be humble about that, mustn't we? Humility is so important."

Again the electrically operated smile, and the nervous glancing here, there, and everywhere.

"I am not sure," said Lamiel, "that there is any necessary connection between the virtue of humility and the refusal to believe. Brought up in less up-to-date circles, I was early trained to see a connection rather between pride and the rejection of faith. But continue, pray. You have explained 'Tentative.' Why 'Theological Technology'?"

"Yes...er...well, now," said Dr. Primrose. "This is one of our most interesting and, I believe, most fruitful phrases. It opens the door to new contacts and sympathies between Churchmen and men of a more practical bent..."

"Really," said Lamiel, "I cannot allow to go unchallenged this extraordinary antithesis between Churchmen and practical men. Are you implying that Churchmen are necessarily unpractical?"

"Well, er...*practical* is a difficult word. We must be careful how we use it. It comes from a Greek word meaning 'to act.' Perhaps I should have said *active*, but that has unfortunate connotations and suggests the reverse of passive...."

"It does indeed," said Lamiel, "but I can see that I must not interrupt you. Pray continue with your original explanation of 'Theological Technology.' "

"Yes, yes...er, of course. We do want to avoid any suggestion that our religion separates us from our fellows, don't we? There's been so much of that kind of thing. The old theologians made such unfortunate distinctions; so watertight, so theoretical, so unreal....We are trying to get beyond all that. We want our religion to be regarded as something that brings us *closer* to others, whatever their beliefs. There's a growing realization—at the higher levels—that all the divisions of the past are out of date. Our theology here avoids making these troublesome academic distinctions. It's a real practical tool for drawing people together; it's a technology that does something of what the Social Sciences do so admirably—fits us into life, in brotherhood with all men, of every race and creed."

"And what are the theoretical and academic divisions which you deplore?" asked Lamiel, "for I strongly suspect that you refer to such highly practical matters as the distinctions between the regenerate and the unregenerate, the baptized and the unbaptized, the saved and the damned."

"Oh, come, come!" said Dr. Primrose, obviously shocked. "We must be careful how we use these most misleading words. Really it is better if we don't use them at all; for they have the most unfortunate associations with outworn superstitions. *Salvation* is a case in point. It comes from a word meaning 'health.' I do not like the modern derivatives at all...er...I always speak of *mental health* myself. I think all our members do. We recognize the dangers of pressing home archaic ideas. No, *mental health* is so much safer than *salvation*. It puts the discussion on the right intellectual level, doesn't it? It prevents misunderstanding."

"I should have said myself," Lamiel replied, "that it destroys all possibility of understanding."

"Yes," said Dr. Primrose, "yes, er...I think you and I are really saying the same thing. It's a question of words. I'm sure we agree at bottom."

"Apart from the fact that where I say *understanding* you say *misunderstanding*, there is of course complete unanimity upon one point."

"Exactly," said Dr. Primrose, "and that is the kind of unanimity we must seek. It's so much better than all the old bickering and controversy."

"I cannot deny," said Lamiel, "that you have hit upon a technique for making controversy impossible.

Indeed, you are well on the way to making rational communication unattainable. However, I think it might be useful if you were to give my ward some idea of the scope of your studies here."

"By all means.... As you see, we apply ourselves to a severely practical theology, which can unite men across all barriers. The purely theoretical issues...the contentious doctrines of the Incarnation, Resurrection, Atonement and so on...these have no place in theology really. They belong to history. We must be humble about these old legends and myths; not pretending to know what never can be known. We must leave it to the historian to weigh the pros and cons of what actually happened. I make the point to all new members personally. And I must say that we generally succeed in making them really humble. We rarely have anyone who is arrogant and bigoted enough to claim certainty on these questions, which have left the greatest scholars in doubt. We cannot know these things, any more than we can know who created the universe or to what end we were born. So we go humbly forward, studying in patience the proper means of attaining mental health and personal adjustment to the demands of society. We are greatly helped by the psychologists and sociologists. Already we can see the beginnings of a true scientific theology."

"As a matter of interest," said Lamiel, "what purpose do you think is served by this Paradise in which you now live?"

"Well...er...*Paradise* is a difficult word, a very difficult word. One needs a certain amount of specialized knowledge to speak about it. Actually *Paradise* comes from an old Persian word meaning 'Garden.' I can allow the word, used with that connotation. This is a garden certainly, a garden in which living things grow to perfection. We too strive in our humble way to that end."

"And do you leave no room for repentance and forgiveness?"

"Dear me, you use very unfortunate words—words that bristle with difficulties. It is not easy to explain to you. It is a great pity that you have not read Honours Theology at one of our ancient universities. We really were taught to think about words. None of the old slogans went unscrutinized. *Repentance*, you see, has unfortunate associations with neurotic, masochistic states of mind that are not at all encouraged by post-Freudian thinkers. We seek mental health, as I have said; and this means removing guilt-complexes of all kinds. The self must be free from repressions and inhibitions. In that sense, we do encourage repentance. And the state of mental poise achieved is probably akin to that condition of psychological balance which you misleadingly call *forgiveness*. *Forgiveness*, you see, comes from an ancient Arabic word, meaning 'How-do-you-do?' Used theologicially, it describes a state of harmony with the Absolute."

Lamiel suddenly adopted a tone of firm masterfulness, as if he had decided to come to grips.

"You are in charge of what are called theological studies. You spent your life below as a Christian minister. You formerly accepted certain articles of belief. You were in the habit of publicly reciting certain creeds. In view of this—and for the benefit of my ward—I propose to put two clear questions to you. I should prefer you to answer definitely, yes or no; but I doubt whether it is any longer possible for you to utter those words and to mean them. The first question is:

do you believe that God was incarnate in Jesus
Christ?"

"Well, er...you put it very crudely. At the higher
levels, we have learned to avoid such crudities: they
are fit for the vulgar and unlettered, perhaps—but
they ignore the subtleties of advanced scholarship.
Jesus was a great teacher, a very great teacher; the Divine Wisdom was manifested...well, that is, the Divine Wisdom descended upon Him with peculiar
power and—I will not say 'authority'—but with peculiar effectiveness."

"That will do," said Lamiel. "Now for the second
question. Do you believe that Christ rose from the
dead on the third day? Do you believe in the Resurrection?"

"Well, er...we must be careful...we must be
humble....Humility is so important for Christians....We are all Christians here, I hope. So, as I
say, we must recognize our limitations and bow before
the research of the scholars. *Resurrection* is a difficult
word....Of course, something happened, something
very remarkable...we don't quite know what.
...Empty tomb...and strange hallucinations: but the
important thing is that the disciples were utterly
changed—new men. Oh, yes, certainly something
happened. I quite agree with you there."

Lamiel, so ready to talk on most occasions, subsided
into silence. For the present he seemed to regard the
situation as one to which he could not fruitfully contribute by further speech. And indeed, I felt that it
was difficult to pin the director down clearly enough
to get to grips with anything; but I summoned the resources of my educational experience and had a shot
myself.

"You use the word *Christian*, Dr. Primrose. What is a Christian?"

"It is a difficult word," said Dr. Primrose. "The utmost care must be exercised in using it, except in a very general sense. We must be humble in our definition. And, above all, we must be charitable. Let me assure you that I think of the word *Christian* as one that unites, not as one that divides. Charity claims that we regard the word as one which draws all men together in brotherhood—the fellowship of all who are striving for a better life, all who sincerely seek to know Reality."

"Why, then," asked Lamiel, "do you trouble to call yourself a Christian? You might just as well call yourself a Mohammedan or a Buddhist."

"I agree...er, I agree absolutely," said the director. "One with all men: that's real Christian Charity, isn't it? How nice that we see eye to eye about the real essentials."

It was at this point that I noticed a startling change in Lamiel's expression. His brow became furrowed, as if in stern concentration; and his eyes were directed in utter fixity upon the small door behind the director's desk, which apparently communicated with some inner office. At any rate, fitful sounds of typewriting could be faintly heard from within.

"Who is in there?" Lamiel asked suddenly in a peculiar grating voice.

"Oh, er...Bugin, my new secretary. An invaluable fellow; most attentive to the work of the Institute; most attentive. I selected him from a host of applicants on an immediate impulse...er, I say that because the fellow is not in the least prepossessing in appearance; but I took an instinctive liking to him.

And how reliable one's intuitions can be in judging persons! What an asset he has proved! Not only is he a faithful servant; but he is also a wise counsellor. His advice upon matters of policy is always worth having. He offers it deferentially, of course, he is most respectful; and touchingly grateful to be treated as an equal. I will have no assertion of authority here."

As the director spoke, Lamiel's gaze remained fixed and concentrated. Once or twice he sniffed searchingly, like a dog upon a scent. At last, as if having reached a decision, he said firmly,

"Call him in!"

"Oh, er...by all means. I should like you to meet him. Pray, don't be prejudiced by his unfortunate appearance."

Dr. Primrose rose, opened the door and motioned to someone within. There emerged a slight figure, most surely unattractive in appearance. His face was wrinkled, and disfigured by two great scarlet blotches. He was distinctly hump-backed too. But I had little time for further observations upon him; for, as his eyes met Lamiel's he dropped the great ledger he was carrying with a sudden, startled cry. It crashed to the floor and, leaping over the director's chair, the fellow dashed in panic through the door into the corridor. Lamiel already had the telephone receiver in his hand.

"After him!" he said to me, curtly and firmly. "Keep him in sight. Help will be with you in a moment. Fordshaw 0202...."

I heard no more. I was running down the corridor in chase, and a moment later leaping down the stone staircase three steps at a time. I trusted that Bugin would make for the door, and I continued my headlong descent of the steps, even when he was lost to sight round the bends ahead of me. And I was not mistaken. Out in the street I caught up with him and grabbed his arm. He did not resist, and perhaps this made me unduly confident of my prey. I stared around, wondering what to do with him, and saw the figure of Lamiel at a top-floor window. He made a gesture of approval and then pointed down the road behind me. I looked round and saw a long blue car approaching. At that moment, as I turned, the secretary gave a sudden jerk which sent me sprawling on the pavement. As I struggled to my feet, I saw him take a superhuman leap, which landed him safely on the back of a passing lorry. "Quick!" said a voice behind me: there was a hand at my elbow, and I was bundled into the blue car—but not before I had seen the words *Hierarchical Police* painted on the door.

We gave chase; but somehow there was little excitement in the air. Indeed, I felt as though the experience, bewildering as it was, had already exhausted itself. This was partly due to my irritation at having lost my grip of the fellow through sheer carelessness. It was due also to the fact that the two uniformed gentlemen, who sat before me in the front seats, treated the case as hopeless.

"The only hope was to keep hold of him," said one.

"It was," said the other. "As soon as we get out of the traffic, he will have his coat off."

The lorry was driving at a headlong pace now, weaving in and out of the traffic so neatly that it was difficult for us to keep it in sight.

"Why should he take his coat off?" I asked.

"Why, indeed?" echoed the officer who was driving.

"He'll soon see, won't he?" said the other, with undue sarcasm, I thought.

I did see, however, all too quickly. No sooner had we left the thick traffic behind and gained something like an open road, than the secretary, who had stood tottering drunkenly on top of loaded sacks, hurriedly tore off his coat and, with a sudden leap, flew upwards into the sky.

"Oh!" I exclaimed, taken aback at my own stupidity and carelessness. "And I thought he was a poor hunchback."

This artless confession provided a seemingly endless source of amusement for my companions as we drove back to the Institute.

"The poor hunchback!" one would say, and then both would laugh aloud, repeating in turn, "The poor hunchback!" as if to remind themselves why they were laughing, and to ensure against any cessation of the gaiety. I was a little offended at their rudeness, and only too relieved to be deposited at the door of the Institute again, even though I had to return to Lamiel as an ignominious failure.

When I entered the director's office again, I was astonished to find Dr. Primrose alone. He sat, as before, at his desk, and was nervously tapping a blotting-pad with his fingers.

"My Guardian..." I began, in some dismay.

"He has gone. He left rather hurriedly. He said he had an urgent matter to attend to."

"Didn't he leave a message for me?"

"Yes. He said you would see him again shortly. Meantime you are to make your acquaintance with the Institute. I think I can...er...look after you;

though I shall suffer some immediate discomfort in being deprived of my excellent secretary."

"Don't you realize what he was?" I asked, with unjustifiable scorn, in view of my own failure.

"He was a very good secretary. I know that. He came with the strongest possible recommendation from the Society for Cultural Relations—a much-maligned body, which is doing a wonderful Christian work."

"He was a devil."

"Yes, yes." Dr. Primrose smiled indulgently, and added ironically, "You saw him fly up into the sky, I imagine."

"I certainly did."

"Well, well, you do not surprise me. We have had many a fresher here with much more startling stories than that to tell. And...er...if I may speak confidentially, the company you came in is not the best possible recommendation in our eyes....No, no. I shall not abuse professional etiquette. I am on the best of terms with the members of the Hierarchy—more especially with one or two at the higher levels. We understand each other's work. But the Guardians, you must appreciate, have not had the educational advantages of their superiors. They are naturally prone to superstition. Their influence on this Institution has not been considerable, but it has almost always been unfortunate. Occasionally it has cost us a very promising member. More often, I am glad to say, it is the weaker brethren who succumb to their glib dogmatism. This is an influence which we have to counter persistently in our daily work. And I may say that we achieve a very large measure of success. Of course, we on the staff are men of experience. Many of us spent our lives below in the struggle against superstition."

In order to excuse my silence in the face of Dr. Primrose's assertions, I must explain that there was a peculiar irresistible quality about his utterances. I do not mean that they were convincing by their cogency and persuasiveness. Far from it. Whenever he opened his mouth, I was quite sure that I utterly disagreed with him from the depths of my soul. It wasn't his argument that defeated one: it was the prevailing assumption behind his argument—an assumption manifested in his choice of words, his manner of speaking and his tone of voice—that his auditor accepted his own presuppositions. For instance, you couldn't reply to this last statement of his without uncovering and destroying the antisupernaturalist prejudices upon which all his utterances were based. But these antisupernaturalist prejudices he never argued about: he *assumed* that everyone shared them. He spoke as though they were axiomatic—as though it would be indecent, or at least highly discourteous, to question them. You were made to feel that you could disagree with him openly only by replies which would cast insulting and uncharitable aspersions upon the very foundations of his intelligence. I do not know whether this was cunning in him, or stupidity: perhaps it was a mixture of both. Certainly it made communication extremely difficult. So too did his habit of agreeing with statements which basically contradicted his own beliefs. For I rarely heard him give the lie to anyone. When firmly and openly contradicted, he would shake hands, in cordial agreement, and express pleasure that the difference was only, after all, a matter of words.

All this went through my mind as I heard him now

sliding from one falsehood to another. I recalled that Lamiel had been less talkative than usual in his presence. And I began to wonder whether Dr. Primrose's intellectual position—or rather, his attitude—was one which reason could never touch. I was inclined to think so. There was nothing to get to grips with. There seemed to be only two alternative ways of responding to him; either to tell him flatly that he was talking nonsense, or to keep silence. In the former case one felt guilty of uncharity, arrogance and pride. In the latter case, silence before him left one with an uncomfortable feeling of being committed to guilty acquiescence in falsehood. In short, he put one in the wrong. There was no way out. I began to hate the man. And this gave no satisfaction; for there was something in his timid furtive eyes which seemed to challenge hatred. Perhaps it was what he most desired.

"I am glad," he said, "that we are within reach of agreement on this matter."

"Oh, no," I interrupted.

"Well...er...the little difficulties will soon disappear, when we get down to practical work together. You must go just where you like here. We have no rules and regulations. We are all equal. The teaching staff are elected by the student body; and I hold my own position through election by the staff...er....One of the reasons why I am so sorry to lose Bugin is that he had hit upon a most workable little plan for ensuring that the annual elections should go well....It is so important to have the right leadership at the top, isn't it? Things can become very uncomfortable and disagreeable unless there is really sympathetic and humble leadership."

There was a knock at the door, and a tall, sturdy, florid man entered, beaming jovially.

"Ah," said Dr. Primrose, introducing us. "This is Archdeacon Templecombe, who is in charge of our sociological work. An eminently practical man; the guide, philosopher and friend of many a newcomer. Are you willing to show our visitor round, Archdeacon? No one is more fitted for the task."

The archdeacon slapped his hands together and continued to beam.

"By all means. At your service, sir. We have a pretty piece of organization to show you. No lack of funds to hold up the great work, eh, Dr. Primrose? Plenty of stout hearts and willing hands. You'll find a good spirit and no slacking. Ha, ha, Primrose, the Church is awake here, what!"

I was weary of talk, and I could barely summon a smile. It seemed hard, to be consigned to the garrulous and boisterous archdeacon, when I longed only for peace and quiet.

7

At long last I was left alone—conducted to a comfortable Common Room by the archdeacon and deposited in a roomy armchair. My guide was profuse in unnecessary apologies as he took his leave. I smiled faintly, stretched out my legs, threw back my head and closed my eyes. My brain was in a dazed and surfeited condition. I felt as though I had looked inside every room on every floor of the massive building. I had listened to hundreds—was it thousands?—of descriptions, explanations and anecdotes. I was far too exhausted to attempt to gather together my impressions for the purpose of making a general judgment on the place. I wanted to think about something else. I suppose that was why I turned my head sideways, stretched out my hand and picked up a newspaper from the low table beside my chair. It was the *Paradise Post*, and I glanced at its contents lazily.

The paper was half-covered by advertisements, which told me much that I had already learned. I was urged once more to anoint my engine with Glusol, and to allow Dolores to fit me out with the latest fashions. An eminent Fordshavian artificer, hugely photographed on page three, assured readers that, in putting the finishing touches to a pair of pearly gates, commissioned by the Hierarchy, he had polished only with Starbright Toothpaste. From this my eyes moved to a gossip column—

SIDELIGHTS FROM DOWN UNDER

The cutest, loveliest thing in this season's catch dropped into my office today.

Said she: "I give you three guesses."

Said I: "One only, thank you. Spotlight Sadie!"

"Bang on, first time. Sadie in person. Hot from Hollywood to Heaven at the age of thirty-five."

The most devastating eyebrows in the film-world lifted quizzically; and I steadied myself with a drink. It isn't every morning that the screen idol of a fellow's youth is served up on a plate with the elevenses. Regaining consciousness, I coolly took stock of the notorious hips, the twenty-one-inch waist, and the slate-blue eyes that knocked up half a billion for Multicolour Inc. Sadie in the flesh all right—and what flesh!

I put the usual: "How did you pass over?"

"Accidental Death. We left by strato-cruiser for Paris and took the wrong turning."

I grinned. "You've reached the right place."

"I guess you'll be seeing quite a few of us around. Hollywood has gone religious. Nothing sentimental. And not an advertising stunt this time. Just plain boredom doing its work. *Are you saved?* That's the question now: it pops out over a glass of champagne and, before you know what you're doing, you've teamed up for Sharing Parties with the United Christian Stars. So here I am."

Which only goes to show that it's true.

I've been shouting my head off about it in this column for weeks.

AND IT'S TRUE.

Call it what you like: Rebirth, Revival, Wholesale
Conversion. Only call it something. You've got to.
'Cause it's happened. They're waking up down under.
And they're waking up to something big.

Watch out for more news, folks.

The paper saddened me. I put it down and stared
round the room. It was a large room, which managed
at the same time to look cosy. The ceiling was low, for
one thing. There was a thick carpet, and dozens of
armchairs arranged in little groups around convenient
coffee tables. One or two people sat dozing or reading
magazines. A man at the far end got up, looked at his
watch, and switched on the radio. I leaned back again
and closed my eyes, glad to be distracted from thought
by the strains of sentimental cafe music. The band was
overbalanced by an excess of strings. The violins
larded a 'cello melody with chromatic harmonies, du-
plicated in the higher registers. I crossed my legs and
waved a foot in sympathy.

It didn't last for long. An unctuous voice bade us *au
revoir* against a fading musical background. There
was a brief silence. Then a record of *The Girl I Left
Behind Me* introduced another speaker.

"Hands across the Grave; our weekly programme of
contacts with the folks we have left behind. Listeners
with requests for this programme should send them,
on postcards please, to Hands across the Grave, Fordshaw Broadcasting Company, Fordshaw. May I say, as
usual, please, that the F.B.C. cannot undertake to answer enquires about whether broadcast messages have
been received down below. We put out these programmes on high-frequency transmitters; but we cannot guarantee that they are received. The number of
sensitive receivers down below is small. But do not hes-
itate to send us your messages. A medium on the Earth

may be listening to us even now. Your own husband or son may be eagerly waiting at a seance. This is your one weekly chance to stretch out your Hands across the Grave."

After a few bars of *Home, Sweet Home*, the announcer began again:

"Before we broadcast our own messages of hope and comfort, here are one or two messages received by our Listening Panel from mediums on Earth contacted during the past week.

"First a message to Susie from Enid. The names were clearly enunciated. The message reads—*We have not forgotten you. Herbert has won two thousand on the Pools. New carpets all round. We're so happy.*

"And here is a message to Jolyf, or it may be 'Johnny'—from Jeremy, or it may be 'Cher and me.' There is a little doubt about the exact wording of the message. It sounded like—*Keep a stiff upper lip. All over now*. But it may be—*Keith is stiff; got stuck up a lift. All over now.*

"And lastly, here is a message which has caused us some difficulty. It is clearly addressed to Doodles, and comes either from 'Chrysanthemum' or from 'Chris and the Mum.' The wording appears to be—*Dad is picking up. Frisky's had kittens. Only two of each. Goodnight now*. But it may possibly be rendered—*Daddy's given up whisky and bitters. Only two of each at night now.*

"And now for this week's requests from listeners at home. Mrs. Mabel Follifoot asks us to send her love and best wishes to her folks, the Follifeet, back in Liverpool. She would like us to play for them this record of *Meet me in the garden, José*, which will bring back special memories to Sonny and Grandpa."

Music followed, and apparently I fell into a doze, for the next thing I was aware of was a light tap on the

shoulder and that dull ache in the head which usually
succeeds my attempts to sleep during the hours of day-
light. I rubbed my eyes and opened them upon the
frail figure of Dr. Primrose.

"You have seen...er...something of what we are
doing," he said, darting half-a-dozen shifting glances
in all directions.

"Oh, yes," I said, gathering myself into a more upright position. "The archdeacon was a very thorough
guide."

"I'm so glad. I believe you heard Dr. Schwindhof
lecturing in the Psychology Laboratory. I'm so happy
that you had that opportunity. We are very proud
...humbly proud, if I may say so, of our work in that
direction. We are really unearthing the springs of religious impulse in the subconscious. It is clear to us now
that the...er...dogmatic, authoritarian approach to
religion is the direct result of a particular set of psy-
chophysical antecedents. When the early child-parent
relationship develops under a dominating father-pres-
sure, a demand is stimulated in the subconscious
which may persist for a lifetime; the demand for an
authoritarian father-pattern, which confines religious
experience within the mould of a rigid dogma. This
discovery is important to us in our attempt to get at
the real meaning behind the rigid dogmatism which
does so much damage to the personality. We make
rapid progress...and our results are promising. We
can already point to the hereditary and environmental
factors responsible for all the varieties of religious em-
phasis—ritualistic and evangelistic, dogmatic and ethical—which have split Christendom in the past. This
is the real road to unity, isn't it?—the humble road to
unity. So much more fruitful than all the old obses-

sions with feasts and fasts, rites and ceremonies, sacraments and doctrines. Psychology is showing the way. We are on the brink of a great new understanding between the psychologists and the true theologians. Of course, the theologians will have to meet their opposites half-way. They will have to grant that human behaviour is a natural phenomenon: but there are few so superstitious as to deny that nowadays. Yes, we can look forward to a great rapprochement. The psychologists are getting there: a little more research on the conditioned reflex and the thing should be settled. Psychology and Christian Theology will be two names for the same subject."

"It is most interesting," I said, feeling too weary for an argument, which would need a patient analysis of first principles with a man who could not listen. And then, conscious of guilty acquiescence, I added, "But it's not true."

"No, no, not yet...but it soon will be. You're quite right; it soon will be. A little more research, that's all. We must be patient, and humble...er....Did you see anything of our work on language?"

"I looked into your Linguistic Department," I said. "Some discussion was going forward."

"Good, very good. I'm so glad. It is such important work. We have a strictly scientific course, designed to eliminate the emotive and metaphorical elements from the language of religious statement. For metaphor stands in the way of unity. It splits up the Great Church into sects and parties. We try to rationalize religious doctrines by cutting out the metaphorical overtones which interfere with clear thinking. The doctrine of the Resurrection, for instance. It is so difficult to accept, isn't it, if one adopts the metaphor of a person actually rising in some kind of body from a physical death. But exclude the metaphorical element, and the meaning of the doctrine is clear and universally acceptable. It is simply a doctrine of Renewal. From the experience of earthly privations and sufferings, man must be renewed, sharing in that gift of Divine Renewal which is so beautifully—but so confusingly—symbolized for us in the legend of the Resurrection. That is why we always speak here of the doctrine of the Renewal. You will get used to the word."

"It has its metaphorical overtones too," I said. "It makes me think of taking my library book back at the weekend, for the purpose of avoiding a fine."

"Yes, yes. The beauty of the word is that it allows each of us to put his own felicitous interpretation upon it without any necessary reference to a superstitious myth. We are getting rid of the idea that such myths need to be imposed upon all. The core of meaning which they conceal is being restated in clear, abstract terms, free of mystical associations. The doctrine of the Incarnation, for instance. What more easy to accept, when you have cleaned away the metaphor of a God actually born as man of the flesh of a Jewish Maiden? Of course, it is beautiful; but it makes a true understanding with the rationalists impossible. And there are so many really Christian rationalists, determined to live a good life. No: we must see the inner meaning of the legend—the truth that the nature of the Eternal Reality was expressed in the life of a great Teacher, and may be expressed in the lives of each one of us."

"Downright heresy," I said, wearily and in every sense weakly. The will to argue was moribund.

"Yes, yes," said Dr. Primrose triumphantly. "How right you are! The heresies of today shall unite in the great new orthodoxy of tomorrow. You have hit the nail on the head....And now I want to show you another department, of which we have reason to be proud...er...humbly proud. It is a new venture for us, but it is making great headway. We have set it to work in a building across the road: for we are sadly overcrowded here."

He rose, and I rose too. Then a thought struck me.

"Ought I to go away from here? I understood that Archdeacon Templecombe was to rejoin me in this room later. I don't want to be rude."

"No, no. It's quite all right. I should have explained to you. A sudden surprise has detained the archdeacon...a most unexpected event, but...er...very agreeable. Mrs. Templecombe has arrived here. We had no idea she was on her way. She appeared in the building a short while ago, accompanied by another new arrival, a Mr....er...Packet."

"Racketts," I said.

"Yes, Racketts. A most interesting gentleman. He says he is anxious to join us here. I'm sure it can be arranged. No candidate who was really anxious to join us here has ever been refused permission. I think that shows how favourably we stand in the view of those above. We are very grateful for the support given to us by the Hierarchies. Of course, there are occasional misunderstandings between ourselves and the ordinary working Angels, but our efforts are really appreciated at the higher levels. I'm sure of that."

We walked towards the door, and Dr. Primrose began straightaway to explain the nature of the new enterprise which I was to visit.

"The plan arose out of the last full meeting of the Institute some nine months ago. As you know, very many of us here are Churchmen, clergy and laity, with a wide collective experience of parish work below. We began to feel that the resources of our collective experience ought to be tapped for some constructive purpose. We decided that it was incumbent upon us to reflect upon what we learned in our work below, and to pool this wisdom bred of practical experience—for the benefit of others. It occurred to us that some kind of formal Report, giving advice about the work of evangelization in the modern world, could be drawn up from the fruits of our combined experience. Such a Report, involving practical recommendations for the conversion of the modern world, will surely prove of inestimable advantage to our brothers down below."

"How will it reach the brothers down below?" I had to shout my question, for we were now walking up the High Street and the traffic was unbearably noisy.

"Ah, yes...er...that is a most natural question. I didn't mean to suggest that our report would be directly communicated to men on the Earth. Our aid will, of course, reach them indirectly. We intend to submit our Report to the higher authorities in the Hierarchies, with a request that it be brought to God's notice. We are determined to help God. He needs our help. Let us admit that things are not going very well with His cause down below just at present. All the greater reason why we should come forward with our advice. This Report will show our genuine willingness to assist God, in an advisory capacity, as indeed we are best fitted to assist. As a list of sound recommendations, based on first-hand practical experience, the

Report will surely be an invaluable guide to God. We realize that He must find the modern mind rather bewildering, and we will design this Report as a kind of reference book, which will throw useful light upon the complexities of the contemporary scene. We simply wish to share our own special insights. The whole scheme is really an act of charity, humbly performed. Of course, it may be argued that we have not ourselves received here benefits from above of a kind to justify this gesture; but we refuse to limit our gifts in a niggardly fashion, making them merely commensurate with what we have received. And indeed we hope that our gesture will bring some response...er...some special recognition...er...some concrete indication that our work is appreciated. Perhaps it is not too much to hope that our Institute may be given a new charter, more befitting its dignity and achievements....That has been in our minds....We should dearly like to have our Institute freed from all angelic control. We are hampered, as perhaps you have realized, by inconvenient visitations. Your Guardian's intrusion here today is a case in point. These intrusions are not helpful: we have to waste time in explaining things to ordinary working Angels who are not really equipped to understand. Our labours would be more fruitful if we had direct contact with the Central Office...er...let us cross here."

We darted through the dangerous traffic, pausing a moment to recuperate on an island in mid-stream. Once safely ashore at the other side, Dr. Primrose led me through the main door of a large block of offices. He pointed proudly to a painted wooden board, tucked among a dozen others, which read—

I.T.T.T. COMMISSION FOR WORLD CONVERSION.
4th Floor

"Let us climb the stairs," he said. "I take little exercise."

We mounted a solid, iron staircase which ran round the four sides of the lift shaft. On the fourth floor we turned on to an iron balcony, running around the three sides of a rectangle. Below us were three more such balconies and then the floor of the entrance hall: above us one more balcony and then a pointed dome-like roof of green frosted glass. We entered through one of the various doors at the side of the balcony and found ourselves in a long room equipped with several tables on trestles, several filing cabinets, cupboards and sets of pigeonholes. It looked for all the world like a Food Office. A tall, sleek-looking cleric, with papers in one hand and pipe in the other, came forward to greet us.

"This is Canon Sprodin," said Dr. Primrose; and my hand was suddenly clenched firmly in a vicelike grip, my palm being pressed painfully against the bowl of a burning pipe.

"How do you do," said the canon. He smiled a genial, patronizing smile, his head being drawn erectly back against his collar, as if he wished to survey effectively some creature much smaller than himself. Folds of loose flesh crumpled themselves between his jacket and his cheeks. He was an amiable-looking fellow. The weak, receding chin gave him an ingenuous appearance, further emphasized by the downward curve of his eyebrows, which sagged comically from nose to cheek. His dark hair was smoothly plastered back from a shiny sloping forehead; and the forehead's slope and shine were artistically imitated in the line of his ample stomach and the sheen of his stock.

"Canon Sprodin," said Dr. Primrose, "has taken full charge of the Commission's researches."

"I am supported by a wholly admirable staff," said the canon, rather grandly, waving his pipe towards the various figures, male and female, who were seated at stools before the tables, engaged in writing and rubberstamping. "We have a thoroughly good spirit here. Nothing mechanical or impersonal. I make a special point of cultivating the I-Thou relationship with each one of them. Friend Buber has got something there, hasn't he?"

"I think our visitor would like to see...er... something of what the Commission is doing."

"By all means."

The canon beamed, and extracted a drawer from a huge filing cabinet.

"This cabinet is devoted to a sociological analysis of the main profession-groups, trade-groups, and income-groups who are at present not being touched by the Christian Message. This particular drawer, for instance, sums up the special problem of appealing to the middle-income-bracket-technologist. He just hasn't been catered for by the modern Church. We're determined to put down all we know about him— tastes, education, social habits, housing background, family life—then we shall be in a position to recommend some technique for touching him. This is a humdrum file to look at—but it's packed full of living truth about our brothers down below. See—divorce statistics, size of families, percentage possessing cars. This isn't a dead paper record: no false objectivization here, as Friend Berdyaev would say. Real human facts."

I tried to look interested in the contents of the file.

"You have at your fingertips, in one drawer," said the canon, "the life story of today's middle-income-bracket-technologist. You can see at a glance what his average expectation of life is, what his typical social background is like, how much he drinks and smokes, and how much he spends on gambling. You can see what percentage of his class get divorced, what percentage run cars, and what percentage buy television sets. Here, for instance, you see that the married-middle-income-bracket-technologist has an average family of .95 children. Compare it with this," he said, taking out another drawer, and searching the file. "This is the married-upper-income-bracket-council-house-industrial-proletarian. He has an average family of 2.73 children."

He pointed to a row of large leather-bound volumes in an open bookcase by the side of the cabinet.

"This Cross-reference Index enables us to make these comparisons upon any point in question."

He pulled the drawer I was examining from under my hands and began to search it.

"Suppose we are interested to compare the two classes thoroughly on this question of family life. ...Here we are. Average number of Relations resident with families of married-middle-income-bracket-technologist—.07. You see, he manages to keep his house pretty free of grandparents, uncles, aunts and in-laws. Now compare the married-upper-income-bracket-council-house-industrial-proletarian."

He searched the appropriate file.

"Here it is. Average number of Relations resident...—.9. Think what that means. Every family on an urban council estate in an industrial city has got nine-tenths of a grandma or grandpa about the house. We find a higher figure still in the home of the lower-income-bracket-slum-fringe-proletarian. And among the lowest-paid agricultural labourers, I believe there's something like one and a quarter of in-laws personnel to cope with at home. It's revealing, isn't it?"

I said rather weakly that it was. And then, attempting to make amends for my lack of effusiveness, asked what conclusions could be drawn from it, relative to the general questions of evangelization.

"Simple!" said the canon, slapping the black silk waistcoat that lay calmly on his stomach. "Specialization; that is the answer. The Church must learn to specialize. There is no parochial or evangelical technique of general and universal applicability. The Church must learn to adapt its approach to the needs of the particular environment. With one population-group the Family Touch will not work; with another it will. Our Report will make clear just where the various modern appeals to the religious impulse are respectively appropriate. The Happy Home line, which is meat and drink to some, is anathema to others. Again, it's no good shooting the Self-immolation line in a parish which is crying out for the Ethical Boost. Too much energy has been wasted in the past by misapplication. I've seen clergy hacking away, without effect, on an Anti-vice platform, when they might have packed the house to capacity with a Social Reform Crusade."

"How is the work progressing on the General Report itself?" asked Dr. Primrose.

"Splendidly—in some ways. Come with me and let me show you."

The canon led us into an inner office, apparently his own private sanctum. It was comfortably furnished with armchairs, and generously littered with ashtrays. He seated us at our ease and produced a large folio volume from a roll-top desk.

"We are working on the first draft now. The date for the first few sections are already to hand. The rest of the material is coming in, fully sifted and organized, day by day. What we need is someone who could write it up really effectively."

"But our friend here is the very man you are seeking," said Dr. Primrose, flashing four smiling glances at me in swift succession.

"You're not suggesting that I should write up this Report," I said, not knowing whether to be pleased or confounded.

"I am indeed," said Dr. Primrose. "And why not?"

"Oh, come, come!" I protested in embarrassment.

"He has considerable experience as a writer," Dr. Primrose went on. "And I may say that he wields a pretty pen."

"No, no..." I began.

"But this is splendid," said the canon. "It is providential. I cannot but believe that you have been sent here in answer to our need. We must be grateful to the Power that watches over us. Let me formally offer you the post of Editor. It is our duty to co-operate with Providence, as Friend Butterfield would say."

"Really I can't undertake it. I'm not equipped."

"Modesty," said Dr. Primrose. "Becoming; but out

of place. We must all be ready to use what talents we have, humbly accepting whatever superiority has been granted to us."

"No," I said, gratified by the compliment, but reluctantly out of sympathy with the whole project. "I mean that I've not got the right ideas."

"Of course you have," said the canon, leaning over me and slapping my shoulders. "And if you haven't, it doesn't matter. The ideas are all provided. All you have to do is to write them up."

"But that's the whole trouble..." I pleaded.

"No trouble at all," said the canon. "The Call has come to you to serve the great Cause. Are you not proud of the opportunity? Remember to Whom the Report will be tendered. It is a privilege we offer you."

"It is indeed," said Dr. Primrose. "Let me ask one question. Are you concerned in your heart for the conversion of the world?"

"Well, of course I am," I said, slightly offended.

"Very well, then, that's settled," said the canon. "You can start work tomorrow."

"No, no, you don't understand," I said—but I was interrupted by the sudden arrival of three persons, who burst noisily into the room: Mrs. Templecombe, the archdeacon and Racketts.

"Here we are," said the archdeacon. "All at home together and on top of the world—in every sense."

"And just in time," said the canon, "to assist us in persuading our friend here to accept the editorship of our Commission's Report."

"He's just the man, I'm sure," said the archdeacon.

"I can recommend him heartily," said Racketts, "for any literary work. He has the gift."

"And," said the canon, "he shall put it at the service

of the Commission for World Conversion."

"He shall, by jove," said the archdeacon.

"But how wonderful!" said his wife. "How I envy you. To be able to write. To be able to express yourself in print. I have always told my husband what a great gift it is. For he too writes, you know."

"Then why shouldn't he edit the Report?" I asked.

There was an awkward pause.

"Well," said the archdeacon. "Truth will out. I'm not a man to pretend to be more than I am. I just haven't got the vivid touch. My stuff is too turgid-...too verbose. We want something extra special for this Report; something distinctive..."

"Something with the real literary flavour," said the canon.

"Something that speaks to the heart," said Dr. Primrose.

"And that's what you've got to offer us," said the archdeacon.

"It is: most certainly it is," said Dr. Primrose.

I looked around at the circle of smiling faces, at the admiring eyes eagerly centred on myself. To reject the appeal of such a friendly group of well-wishers seemed churlish in the extreme. In any case, I was wearied by their importunities and sick of standing in aloof and critical detachment. I blushed and lowered my head a little.

"Very well," I said. "If you put it like that, I'll..."

"You'll what?" thundered an angry, impassioned voice, that shook us all into attitudes of dismay. "You'll what?" And Lamiel strode through the doorway, with a blaze in his eyes that caused me to bury my head in my knees. For a few moments no one uttered a sound or moved an inch. "Angel of Wrath!"—the phrase was hammered out vibratingly in my brain, as though my skull were inhabited by a swinging gong. As Lamiel spoke again, I was conscious that he towered over us in gigantic, inaccessible majesty.

"You are under my guardianship still. It is fortunate for you that you are. You will come with me!"

Without raising my eyes or my head, I slid out of the chair and slunk after him from the room.

8

We walked through the streets of Fordshaw at an uncomfortably rapid pace. Lamiel led me with a determined stride, and said nothing. For a long time I was too afraid to speak. I attributed both Lamiel's haste and his silence to his displeasure. I realized that, in a sense, I had been tested and found wanting. Yet, as I reflected upon what had happened in Canon Sprodin's department, I began to feel that perhaps I was not quite so black as Lamiel judged me. It seemed bad enough that my Guardian should have surprised me on the point of undertaking something which I didn't believe in at all: yet it was even worse that he should be ignorant of the course of events and the train of thought which had brought me to that point. I became determined to speak—if not in self-defence, at least in clarification of what had actually taken place.

"I don't want to defend myself," I began nervously.

"I think you do," said Lamiel curtly.

There could be no reply to this. Once more the hackneyed, half-meant conversational opening had made me look a fool. I realized that, whatever explanation was to be given, it would have to be framed exactly and with scrupulous honesty.

"I mean," I said, "that I'm not going to try to exculpate myself."

"That is at least sensible," said Lamiel, "for indeed any such attempt would be useless."

"Yes," I went on, "but I should like to explain exactly what happened."

"Do you think that is necessary?"

"I do, as it happens. It is possible that your picture of my behaviour is not quite the same as mine."

"It is more than possible: it is highly probable—to judge from your opening remarks."

"Really you are making it very difficult for me to speak about this matter."

"That is my intention," said Lamiel.

"Does it help, to confuse me at the outset? I mean, wouldn't it be better to hear me to the end?"

"I'm not sure," said Lamiel. "I suspect that it may be better to stop you at the beginning. It all depends what you are going to say. However, if you insist, I will listen."

"Well, then, I admit that I was flattered into lending my services to the Commission."

"That is so."

"But vanity was not the only cause. As those people argued with me and tried to persuade me, I felt every minute more and more conscious of cutting myself off from them—by resisting, I mean."

"Yes, I understand perfectly."

"I felt that I was being bigoted, aloof, unhelpful and—well, to put it bluntly, uncharitable."

"So," said Lamiel, slowly and deliberately. "You began to identify acquiescence with charity."

"Yes. That's what I mean. I was wrong, I suppose."

"You were."

"But you see how it happened?"

"One moment," said Lamiel, "for this is a difficult point. You are arguing that your acquiescence was motivated, not only by vanity, but also by a false view of charity?"

"Yes, that's it."

"And you agree that this view of charity was an erroneous one?"

"I'm ready to admit it."

"In that case," said Lamiel, "the substance of your explanation amounts to this: that you were guilty not only of sin but of error too. I see now what you meant when you suggested that my picture of your case might be different from your own. You were afraid lest I had judged you too leniently, being aware of your moral failing, but ignorant of your erroneous judgment. You may set your heart at rest. I have overestimated neither your moral nor your intellectual capacities."

I was silent. This conclusion was not what I had sought: but there seemed to be something unassailable about it. The intention which set me explaining had somehow been dissipated by the logic of the argument. And I did not feel anxious to recover it. We walked at a steadier pace now, and I felt less oppressed and worried, though even more desolate. Suddenly Lamiel took up the subject again.

"What was your candid opinion of the work of the Commission for World Conversion?"

"That it was worthless."

"So that there could be no exercise of true charity in

your assisting the work or encouraging others to pro-
ceed with it?"

"No."

"And this was your view at the time, so that you
were reluctant to undertake the editorial work?"

"Yes, indeed."

"It appears," said Lamiel, "that you never seriously
indulged the intellectual error of confusing acquiescence with charity."

"I didn't think it out rationally. I just had a feeling,
after a time, that it is better to get on with people than
to be at odds with them."

"Ah. We have misjudged the case. There was no intellectual error, strictly speaking, after all. There was
just a feeling. Now, feelings cannot be true or false.
They can only be good or bad, appropriate or inap-
propriate. Perhaps we ought to investigate this feeling."

I began to be extremely uncomfortable again, as
Lamiel went on remorselessly.

"I suggest that this feeling—which we have errone-
ously associated with charity—was, in fact, a desire to
feel comfortable in the presence of others, a desire to
be liked and to be admired by others, even though
these others were wholly concerned to serve ends
which you considered to be bad. In short, here is vanity again, if I am not mistaken; a vanity to which you
were prepared to sacrifice principles, and a vanity
which you were prepared to disguise as charity. You
stand exculpated of innocent intellectual error. But
the moral picture does not improve under analysis.
Perhaps we had better leave it at that."

"Yes," I said, feeling oddly relieved that we had at

last reached rock-bottom, "perhaps it would be as well."

"Though I trust," said Lamiel, "that you will learn to be on your guard against feelings, especially when they masquerade as impulses of charity. The exercise of charity is the work of the will. I am afraid that there are circumstances in which the exercise of charity will have an uncompromising, unsociable, even disagreeable appearance. I believe that neither Dr. Primrose nor yourself has found me at all times a congenial companion. There may be something for you to learn from that."

9

"Before you face your second tribunal," said Lamiel, "you ought to get your head clear about what
you have seen and heard. Out here we have an excellent opportunity for reflection and conversation."

We sat at a wooden table in the garden of a little
country inn, miles away from the noise of Fordshaw,
and as far from the fussiness of Helicon. In Lamiel's
tone was expressed the readiness to talk at leisure and
without irony. I was pleased at the prospect of tranquil discourse, but I felt more eager to listen than to
speak; and I said so.

"For I am too confused to make a sensible contribution."

"I am not sorry to hear you say so," said Lamiel.
"No doubt it is better that I should try to bring clarity
to your reflections and conclusions."

"But there is just one thing, before you begin," I
said, "—one question which I should like you to answer. This country—the region of Helicon and Fordshaw—is it Purgatory or Hell?"

"It is both, in a sense. In terms of sin and wretched-
ness and isolation, it is Hell. But since neither of us

knows for how many of its inhabitants it has the finality of Hell, we shall do better to call it Purgatory."

"Thank you," I said. "That answers my question. Indeed, I believe it answers all my questions."

"I don't think it does. You know now, as far as you can know, what this place is: but you do not know how it comes to be. Nor do you know what other cities there are for the reception of the dead—cities whose inhabitants are clothed in glory. Yet your own experiences on earth must have led you to believe in far different inheritances beyond the grave than are enjoyed in the cities you have visited. No doubt you have known many a taste below of the frustrations, fatuities and faithlessnesses of Helicon and Fordshaw. But you have also seen, here and there in your earthly career, a hint of some more abiding city, built in such light and glory that it has no need of any sun, neither of the moon to shine in it."

"I have not been entirely forgetful of this," I said. "I have realized all along that far different cities must exist here."

"How could you forget? You have not met your own parents in Helicon or Fordshaw; nor could you expect to. You have not met any of those whose example and teaching gave you most to admire and emulate on earth below. You have seen in Helicon and Fordshaw poor erring sheep, clergy and laity, in whom the eye of faith is dim or blind. But you have not seen there any of the faithful priests and laymen whom you knew for their works of mercy and words of enlightenment, and whom you marked for their lives of prayer and praise."

"I realize," I said, "that I have not seen in these cities the Church, as She is. Indeed, I have not really seen the Church at all here. How could I expect to, in the places I was especially condemned to visit?"

"That is true. Yet I must remind you of all that it means. Your experience in these places is the best possible incentive to self-analysis. Used thus, it can only be beneficial to you. But the same experience would be the worst possible basis for judgment upon the Church—or other institutions—down below. Used for that purpose, it would corrupt your soul."

"Unless it were counterbalanced by some vision of the Church in those more abiding cities, of which you have spoken."

"For obvious reasons, that vision has not been granted to you."

"But I have read of it in the works of others," I said. "There are some whose words will not let you rest, for the yearnings they stir and the glimpses of glory they bring before your eyes—

> The steadfast rest of all things, firmly stayed
> Upon the pillars of Eternity."

"It is good that you have read these things. But it is one thing to read of the Glory, and another thing to approach it in the mystery of prayer and the practice of holiness."

"I think I have sometimes actually approached the Glory, else how should I have known the word for truth, when I read it? I do not mean that I ever learned to approach it in the disciplines of prayer and holiness: but down below there are lesser vehicles for the revelation of what always is, in splendour and light. As well as priests and prophets, we have our poets. After their own fashion they explore the Way. And any man who loves a woman for herself, or a symphony for its grace and strength—does he not glimpse something of the real Glory? You have yourself spoken of the visions which illuminate life in the flesh. These are not granted only to the regenerate. Surely a revelation is granted to any man who discerns the finger of Glory in the created world. Wordsworth enjoyed and indulged a profound revelation without any religious discipline. He saw hills, rocks and streams as—

> Characters of the great Apocalypse,
> The types and symbols of Eternity,
> Of first and last and midst and without end."

Lamiel paused a little before replying, as if he did not know quite what to say.

"This, I am afraid," he said at length, "is the one subject in the universe upon which you can speak with more authority than I. These lesser vehicles of the Glory are not for us. We do not need them. I do not mean by this that we are better without them; still less that you would do well below to neglect them. I only know that the human heart's incarnate love for the creature of flesh and the creation of dust, is a way to shame and a way to glory which the discarnate soul can never tread."

"That certainly seems to detract from their significance."

"Not at all—for you. These things are among the peculiar graces of human creaturehood. They are a part of the endowment of natural man. And, like all gifts in natural man's endowment, they need to be disciplined by doctrine and obedience, to be transfigured by sacrament and worship. In short, if the fulfilment which they promise is to be realized, there must be the practise of prayer and holiness. Without this, the promises remain only promises, if they remain at all; and hopes continually deferred sicken the heart. Yet in these necessary disciplines you confess yourself unpractised. You did not learn, even from the example of Tony Riddell."

"What is true of man's loves and adorations," I said, "is presumably true of his reasoning too—even his reasoning about the nature of God and the meaning of life. All these activities must suffer a discipline of holiness, or they become at best the mere ornaments and indulgencies of physical man's earthly prosperity. Is that what you mean?"

"Exactly: at best they become just that. At worst, they become the vehicles of degradation into unredeemed sensuality and earth-bound individualism. Surely that is the lesson of Helicon and Fordshaw. There is no natural good which may not become a transfiguring grace in the lives of those who seek holiness, in worship and obedience. And there is no natural good which cannot become a vehicle of degradation in the lives of those whose wills are directed to the service of self. The study of theology and the practise of social reform are, in this respect, no different from the love of man for woman, for art, or for the created world. These things may degrade a man to sensuality: they may exalt him to physical mastery or to intellectual mastery over his fellows and over his environment. But unless they are enjoyed and endured under the discipline of a faith which gives and adores, they cannot fit a man for this life beyond time."

"I am in difficulty here," I said, "for if what you say

is true—as of course it must be—then the unregenerate man who studies theology is really no better employed than the unregenerate man who studies racing form. In the same way, it would seem to follow that the man who asserts his masterfulness in directing a campaign for slum-clearance is no better employed than the man who asserts his masterfulness in organizing a speedway contest."

"Be careful. I did not say that theology was not a better subject to study than racing form. I said merely that the study of theology was not necessarily conducive to spiritual growth. But even in the case of the wholly self-centered and worldly man, the study of theology is more likely to touch the unawakened soul than the study of racing form. As for your other example, it surely needs no explanation. A man may damage his soul as effectively in organizing slum-clearance as in organizing speedway contests: indeed the former activity offers greater opportunities for the growth of spiritual pride and moral self-congratulation. The more potentially fruitful an occupation is, the greater are the opportunities it offers both for the soul's health and for the soul's damnation.

"You have heard that evil is a perversion of the good. The greatest goods can be perverted into the greatest evils. The poor man has not the opportunities for covetousness and self-indulgence which the rich man enjoys. The unlettered man has not the opportunities for intellectual pride and arrogance which the scholar may succumb to. An irreligious man may prostitute the flesh; but it takes a 'religious' man to prostitute the things of the Spirit and the Church of God. Every gift, every insight, every vision, every talent brings its demand for self-forgetfulness in sanctified service: each brings its opportunities for richer worship or for more damnable self-love. The slum labourer may pervert beer and steak to the sole end of abusing an indulged body. It takes a bishop to pervert episcopacy to the service of self-indulgence; it takes a monk to pervert the religious life to the service of pride.

"The deepest regions of Hell are for priests and prophets and teachers who have served the self; for the rich, the gifted and the worldly wise. The poor have a different inheritance. The poorest of all—in spirit, in intellect, in personal charm and personal possessions—have little opportunity for damning themselves."

"It sounds like an argument for the abolition of education," I said.

"It may sound like that; but it certainly isn't that. You must seek below to open up all possible opportunities for good. But you must do so in the realization that they are also opportunities for evil. What precise demands this truth makes upon your earthly educational systems I cannot say. It is *your* business to discover them; and that is your specific educational opportunity, for good or evil. If you do not discover them, your education will be a corruption of the mind and a disintegration of the soul."

"As indeed it all too often is," I said.

"Then you must improve it," Lamiel replied, with more warmth that he had previously shown during the conversation. "Your business is to seek the appropriate discipline for education, whilst others seek the discipline for ownership, statecraft, or artistic creation. The whole argument is directed towards this single conclusion. All these activities must be brought under the disciplines I have mentioned—of doctrine and obedience, of sacrament and worship."

"Is not this," I asked, "another way of saying that man is the child of God and an inheritor of the Kingdom of Heaven—and that all his activities must bear reference to that truth?"

"It is. Man is the child of Nature and, as such, may grow, in the experience of mind and body, to a maturity of animal mastery and well-being. To this end the study of theology or the organization of ecclesiastical affairs may contribute as surely as the pursuit of pleasure and wealth. These pursuits may bring prosperity and prestige, glory in the lordly play of the intellect, delight in the response of sense and emotion, pride in the potency of nod or gesture: but, thus unredeemed, they are death to the soul. For man is the child of Supernature and, as such, must grow in the life of another dimension. He is called to root himself in an order which transcends the finite. From this order he derives his motives; to this order he directs his aspirations; in the light of this order he forms his judgments and makes his choices; through his vision of this order he attains to truth, wisdom and the knowledge of what always and necessarily is. This order is the constitution of that Eternal City where the Will of God is all in all.

"The Christian Religion is the means whereby man learns to live at this supernatural level. In the Faith and teaching of the Church is preserved for you the revelation of this order, and the disciplines by which it may be entered upon, even in the life of the flesh. That the revelation exists in its fullness: this is the gift of the Incarnation. That the supernatural life may be enjoyed and endured by the fallen in flesh: this is the gift of the Redemption and the Atonement. For man it becomes a question of self-committal—to the Will of God, to the authority of the Church which is His Incarnate Body, to the truth of Her Revelation and the efficacy of Her sacramental life. This self-committal is Faith. It is also the practise of the Christian Religion. When Christians cease to practise a religion, or to commit themselves in faith—then you have Helicon and Fordshaw, much talk of God, much ethical uplift, much personal well-wishing, much planning, thinking and doing. But there is little faith, less religion, and hardly a glimmer of obedience or worship. When you understand the plight of Helicon and Fordshaw, you understand much of the tragedy of your own twentieth-century Christendom on earth below. Hell may be there too—even where the duty of man, the mission of the Church and the Christian view of life are much advertised and discussed; even where the name of God is on everybody's lips."

10

Again the long, pillared hall of judgment; the two
rows of silent angelic secretaries; the grave, imper-
turbable President. Again the silent, watchful group
of examinees, huddled forlornly in dim, shadowed re-
moteness from the shining dais. Again the hour or so
of waiting and listening; the periodic summons to Ruziel; the clear, persistent probing of the President's
questions. And in my mind, once more, the faint but
inescapable memory of the end-of-term Collections of
long ago.

Again I responded to my name and stood before the
President: but this time I was not alone. For Lamiel
had appeared through the bottom doorway of the hall
as I made my way to the dais. And now he stood beside me. As an advocate or as a prosecutor? I was not
quite sure. I felt grievously uncertain which role he
would assume. This was not because I did not trust
him; but because I did trust him. I knew he would do
the best for me; and I was not at all sure that I should
like his "best." There were odd surprises always in the
company of Lamiel. His support might turn out to be
some very personal kind of support—some advocacy

after the fashion of frail, human loyalty, which would paint my character, even my weaknesses, in the most favourable light possible. But it seemed more likely that Lamiel would do his best for me in a very different fashion—in some terribly impersonal kind of way: that he would plead, with unflinching angelic clarity, for a harsh discipline upon a shabby and shoddy human spirituality.

"You are ill at ease," said the President gently.

"Yes, sir," I said, making an attempt to pull myself together.

"I think perhaps you forget the limitations of this court. Our direct concern is simply with the matter of your immediate occupation."

It was true. I had been worrying about issues of a much more momentous kind.

"A second examination is very different from a first one," said the President, "in that you are able to speak with some knowledge of our organization here. You now have the advantage of a first-hand acquaintance with some of the departments in the educational system provided for newcomers—newcomers of a certain type, that is. You saw Helicon and the College for Gnostics. Do you think you belong there?"

"I don't know whether I belong there, sir. I hope not. I certainly don't want to go there."

"I see," said the President. "You appear to be clear enough on that point. You have also seen Fordshaw. Do you belong there, in the Backward Believers' Department?"

"I can only give the same reply, sir. I have no wish to go there either."

"You speak with confidence," said the President. "I hope you will be able to reply with equal confidence to my next question. Suppose it is our pleasure to commit you to the one institution or the other; which of the two would you choose?"

This was the question I had most dreaded—of all the questions that might be foreseen. I felt it was a trap; and I knew that there was no escape from it. I was sure that open preference for either could be nothing but a confession of guilt. And yet I was bidden to choose. I was bound to be in the wrong. To this I was brought. Even if I tried to evade the question, by pretending that both were equally abhorrent to me, still I should be in the wrong. For, in the first place, I did not hate both places equally: so that any such evasion would be a lie. And, in the second place, I had been given only the two alternatives—and purposely given only those. The responsibility laid upon me was simply and unmistakably to express a preference. And, in fact, my preference was quite clear to myself. The depths of faithlessness and fatuity in Fordshaw were beyond the depths of Helicon. The vulgarity, the cheapness, the detested 'modernism' of Fordshaw were utterly repellent to me. With all its pretentiousness, Helicon was at least refined. With all its hypocrisy, the place had a glimmer of culture. My answer was predetermined. I knew that there could be no point in delaying its utterance.

"In that case, sir," I said, "I should have to choose Helicon, as the lesser of two evils."

"Helicon is your choice, then," said the President. "All that remains is for me to check up on the reliability of this preference by consulting your Guardian."

He turned to Lamiel.

"Your ward found something to approve in Helicon?"

"I do not think he did," said Lamiel.

"He was, at least, less critical of the place than of Fordshaw?"

"On the contrary, he was alert to the deficiencies of the place from the start."

"He was moved by what he heard in the College for Gnostics, perhaps?"

"No," said Lamiel, quite decisively, "he was critical of what he heard, and made no secret of it."

"He was drawn by the intellectual or personal qualities of people he met there?"

"Not in the least."

"Then maybe," said the President, "he was attracted to some kind of activity there—something to which he felt he could fruitfully contribute?"

Lamiel gave a firm negative again.

"He never showed the slightest sign of any such attraction."

"Ah," said the President. "He wholly disapproved of Helicon. In that case, I must assume that he revealed an even heartier disgust with Fordshaw."

"I am afraid that he did not. On the contrary, he admitted that Helicon might be compared unfavourably with Fordshaw in some particulars."

"You are telling me that he is a liar," said the President; and I saw the first cracks in his patience and imperturbability.

"He noted in Fordshaw," said Lamiel, "some evidence of remorse and repentance wholly absent from Helicon."

"You are telling me," said the President, now visibly angry, "that he prefers to avoid an environment where penitence may seize upon him."

And still Lamiel added fuel to the flames.

"He was fully awake to the impregnable pretentiousness and pride of Helicon. And, although the vul-
garities of Fordshaw displeased him, he was not
unmoved by the personal good-fellowship of Fordshavian enthusiasts. Indeed, there were outward signs of
real sympathy for them in their work."

The President's eyes blazed with indignation. As his
voice rose in a thunder of wrath, I shrank within myself like the shrivelled kernel of a rotten nut. My hands
trembled, and my whole frame seemed to hang loose
about me.

"With this in mind, he now seeks to shun the hand-
clasp of genial vulgarity for the arrogance of refined
hypocrisy."

My desolation was a shattering reality. And yet,
amid all the tremblings and sweatings, amid all that
devastating sense of my littleness, my vanity and my
falsehood, a single thought ran clearly in my mind. It
was this: I could not regret the choice I had made, because it was the choice of the will below the level of
conversational reasoning—below the level of all the
talking and thinking which Lamiel now reproduced
to my utter discomfiture and dismay. Moreover, I
knew with an absolute certainty that, had I made the
alternative choice, preferring Fordshaw, the result
would have been exactly the same. I should have been
brought to precisely the same point of desolation and
humiliation. For the President's wrath was not the
outcome of this immediate decision, not the result of
this recent sequence of experiences—but an inevitable
judgment upon a person. The judgment could have
been no other, unless the person had been other. And
what the person was, here and now, had been settled
in long years of life on earth below. The consciousness

of an inevitable judgment upon what I was, rather than upon what I had said, deprived me of utterance. I was stunned before the final blow.

The President rose from his seat, and towered over me, a mountainous symbol of offended justice and insulted authority.

"May I ask," he said in ringing tones, "what are the full depths of his falsehood?"

There was a brief silence; and then Lamiel said, in his dispassionate, unflinching way—"He was on the point, when I forestalled him, of offering his services as a writer to the Backward Believers' Department."

A deep and deathly calm succeeded this announcement. There was an atmosphere of finality which slightly reassured me. I felt certain now that no worse revelations lay ahead. The attack was over. It was time for the defence. I closed my eyes, determined to hit out forcibly, if unjust recrimination should succeed the tale of justifiable accusations.

I heard the voice of the President, now frighteningly quiet—almost a whisper—"He is capable of that."

And I held my peace and mustered my resources. The point of protest would come, and soon.

It did come. Lamiel's next words reached me as from a remote distance; so detached and impersonal was his tone.

"He is capable of that and more. Were you to despatch him back to Earth at this moment, he would be capable of writing up all this that he has been through in some vulgar and ephemeral book. He would try to make it entertaining, and sell it for profit. And he would pretend to be instructing others in so doing...."

I could bear it no longer; and the long-pent protest burst out.

"No, no, no!" I cried. "No, no!"

There was a pressure on my forehead and a sickening feeling in the pit of my stomach.

"No, no, no!" I repeated, and raised my hand to my oppressed and throbbing head.

An obstacle obstructed my arm. I opened my eyes, and saw my wife leaning over me, her hand keeping down my head on the pillow.

"You are to keep quiet," she said; and I nodded, with a dim sense of relief.

"It was touch and go after the operation. But the doctor has seen you this morning, and there is no doubt now that all is well. It is just a matter of patience now. But you must keep quiet and rest."

I smiled, fully conscious at last of a profound relief, a multifarious relief, whose richness it was going to be a pleasure to explore.